Wendy

Springflower Books (for girls 12–15):

Adrienne
Erica
Jill
Laina
Lisa
Marty
Melissa
Michelle
Paige
Sara
Wendy

Heartsong Books (for young adults):

Andrea
Anne
Carrie
Colleen
Cynthia
Gillian
Jenny
Jocelyn
Kara
Karen
Sherri
Stacey

Mary
Carraway

BETHANY HOUSE PUBLISHERS
MINNEAPOLIS, MINNESOTA 55438
A Division of Bethany Fellowship, Inc.

Library of Congress Catalog Card Number 87–72793
ISBN 0–87123–942–6

Published by Bethany House Publishers
A Division of Bethany Fellowship, Inc.
6820 Auto Club Road, Minneapolis, Minnesota 55438

Printed in the United States of America

Dedicated to
Fount, Flo, Enda,
Thomas, and Simon,
My very own
special family.

MARY CARRAWAY, a high-school teacher for twenty years, has raised two daughters of her own and two foster daughters as well. She is married and makes her home in Mississippi. This is her first book.

Chapter One

"There . . . he . . . is . . . again!" Jane exclaimed. Gasping breaths punctuated her words.

Her oversized sweat shirt, emblazoned with the words *Mountain Falls Track Team*, flapped loosely around her narrow hips as she jogged in place, right there on the corner of Avondale Drive for all the world to see. She had been doing this for the last ten minutes as we waited for the school bus. Even though Jane Olderfield had been my dearest friend since fourth grade, she could really be weird sometimes.

Facing the opposite direction, with my hands casually behind my back, I admired the yellow forsythia bushes in the Camerons' yard and tried my best to pretend that Jane wasn't there.

"Wendy Thomsen!" she yelled at me again. It was impossible now not to turn around and look at her, then scan the familiar street in the direction of her wildly gesturing arms. I looked back at her with a puzzled stare. The most interesting thing in sight was a slinking black cat preparing to make an unsuspecting robin his breakfast. Otherwise the usual 7:30 a.m. quiet of this late-April day was disturbed only by the rhythmic squish of

Jane's sneakers on the pavement and her labored breathing.

"There!" She pointed again and finally came to a standstill, clutching her side and breathing heavily. "That yellow VW with that man in it, in front of your house." She pushed her tousled brown curls back from her high forehead and readjusted her heavy glasses on her small turned-up nose.

At last I saw the car, parked across the street and two houses down from mine.

"So what?" I asked impatiently. "It's just a VW parked on the street. Cars do that, Jane," I reminded her. "And it's not in front of my house. I think it's in front of the Jamesons'."

"Close enough," she retorted. "Do you recognize the car?"

I shook my head.

"Well, neither do I, but it's the third time this week that he's been here."

"How do you know?" I asked.

"Some of us are more observant than others," she remarked in a superior tone of voice. "I've seen him. That's how I know. First I saw him through the window as I was eating breakfast Sunday morning, and yesterday I had to wait for him to drive by before I crossed the street to your house."

It was unusual, but I hated to encourage her. "It's probably just a coincidence," I reasoned. "There must be hundreds of yellow Volkswagens in a town this size."

"But, not on this street and *not* with an Illinois license plate!"

"So what? He's probably a salesman," I suggested. "Insurance or vacuum cleaners."

"Not in this area," she retorted. "No door-to-door salesmen are allowed."

I shrugged and stared down the street again. "Then

maybe he's lost," I concluded.

"For three days?" she asked in disgust. "Come on, Wendy, admit it, there's something strange here and you know it. Do you want to know what I think?"

I knew I really didn't have a choice as she drew herself up to her full five feet six inches (three taller than I). Her thin lips struggled to control a smirk and her hazel eyes narrowed with suspicion.

She leaned her face close to mine and hissed, "I think he's a private detective."

"Huh-uh!" I replied loudly. "Private detectives don't drive around in VW's and besides, what would a private detective be doing on our street?"

A sigh of contempt escaped her lips. "Who knows? Investigating! Detecting! Snooping! Prying! Whatever it is that PI's do. Maybe he's tailing someone. Maybe Mrs. Jameson."

"Maybe he's a dog catcher," I said.

Jane was not amused. "You can laugh, but I'm going to do some detective work of my own."

Before I could stop her, she pranced off down the street in the direction of the mysterious yellow automobile.

"Jane, wait!" I yelled after her. But she tossed her head defiantly and kept walking. This was so typical of Jane, who always rushed into life head-on. I sighed and started after her, pulled her back by the arm, and spun her around.

"Jane, what are you planning to say?" I demanded.

"Simple. I'll just ask him if he's lost and if he needs directions."

Knowing I could not dissuade her, I tagged reluctantly at her heels. Luckily before we reached the car, familiar chugging sounds and the smell of diesel exhaust filled the air as our school bus eclipsed the small car. We sprinted toward the corner, scooped our books from the sidewalk, and scrambled for the door. Jane craned her long neck for one last look before stumbling up the last step of the bus. She clutched at me for support as the heavy vehicle lurched forward.

"Did you see what I saw?" she asked after we had safely plopped into two empty seats.

"I doubt it," I answered honestly.

"You missed his clever disguise?"

"What disguise?" I asked. We never did get close enough to see more than a shiny bald head. "He had a newspaper in front of his face."

"See what I mean? Wouldn't you call that a clever disguise?"

"M-m-m-huh," I mumbled and turned toward the window.

Two whole minutes passed in blissful silence as Jane sulked, and I reveled in the abundance of spring evidenced in deep red tulips, pale crocuses, and golden daffodils complementing the greening grass of carefully landscaped lawns as we drove through Garden Hills subdivision.

The grinding of the engine into a higher gear shook Jane from her pouting.

"You know what your problem is, Wendy? You lack imagination."

"Oh, Jane, you have more than enough for both of us," I chuckled.

"You mark my words," she declared, ignoring my remark. "We haven't seen the last of this mysterious man in the yellow Volkswagen. I think you should tell Dr. Thomsen."

"Why?"

"Because he's home all day, and he could keep his eyes open."

I couldn't argue with that. Dr. Thomsen is my father. The *doctor* is because he's a biology professor. Unlike most fathers, he works at home—in the kitchen, to be precise. Two years ago he published a book on nutrition, which was well accepted, and now he's hooked on health foods. He took a leave of absence from the university to write a cookbook, of all things. The only problem is, he experiments on our family. Lots of fruits, veggies, whole wheat, yogurt, chicken, and fish. It's just that some of his failures are more memorable than his successes. But at least none of us has a weight problem, and we're all so healthy it almost makes people sick.

"He may not be a private detective at all," Jane concluded. "Looks can be deceiving. He may be a crook *masquerading* as a private detective. He's probably casing the houses on our street for a break-in."

Of all the possibilities, this had to be the most absurd, but then I glanced through the window again. The multi-paned windows of the Fabers' Georgian style house gleamed in the sunshine as we drove past. Maybe it wasn't such a farfetched idea. The large homes in our neighborhood would be tempting targets for a burglar.

"And don't forget your mother's paintings," Jane warned. "Good artwork is always a top priority for thieves."

My mother Joanna hasn't painted for several years, not since she opened her own art gallery downtown. Her work is not in the same class as a *Mona Lisa*; however, she is quite well known throughout the Northwest. I shuddered. I had let Jane's imagination run wild with me. Still, the mere thought of some robber staking out my own home raised goose bumps on my arms.

"Can't we talk about something else?" I pleaded.

"OK, but don't say I didn't warn you," she answered smugly. "I don't think we've seen the last of the bald-headed driver of the yellow Volkswagen. And do tell your dad, Wendy," she added earnestly. "I just have this funny feeling."

I felt the same way and promised to follow her advice; then I deliberately changed the subject.

"Did you go to the *Project Outreach* meeting at church last night?"

She nodded. "We made up a list of prospects and then divided the names so we can make some personal contacts." She fished in her purse and handed me a slip of paper. "Here's your assignment."

Hesitantly I unfolded the small square and looked at it and at Jane incredulously.

"Mickey Decker?" I asked with dismay.

"Sure. Why not?"

"Mickey Decker?" I repeated. "I don't even know Mickey Decker."

This was not exactly true. Everyone at Mountain Falls High knew Mickey Decker.

"You sit behind him every day in algebra class," Jane reminded me. "That's a perfect chance to talk to him."

"He doesn't talk to *me*," I lamented. "He's a junior. I'm only a sophomore. Besides . . . you know what he's like."

My mind did an instant replay of Mickey Decker parading down the halls of MFHS. With black eyes, unruly dark hair, faded jeans, tight T-shirts, and a swaggering walk, he was definitely not the fashionable type.

Jane shook her head. "I *don't* know what he's like, and neither do you. You can't judge by hearsay and appearances."

To be honest, I didn't know much about Mickey. In fairness to him, I tried to weigh fact against fantasy. What I actually knew was that his real name was Michael (no nicknames allowed in Mr. Hardy's class); he wasn't much better in math than I was (repeating the class); and he was not Mr. Hardy's favorite student (too many tardies and too few homework assignments completed). Those were the facts. The fantasy was that most of the kids I knew considered him wild and tough. Still, he had never been rude to me in algebra, and that was a fact too.

The squeal of the brakes and a sudden forward jolt signaled our arrival at school. Pushed along by the jostling crowd, Jane and I reached the entrance of the large two-story red brick building.

"What's the worst thing that could happen, Wendy? He's not going to throw rocks at you. You're such a coward. Just invite him to church, that's all. Don't you remember the scripture we studied last week in 2 Timothy, 'God has not given us the spirit of fear, but. . . '?"

". . . of power and love and a sound mind." I remembered. I would claim that promise and pray for both an opportunity and the courage to go with it.

"But you'll have to do it today, Wendy," Jane said as we reached our lockers and put away our books and jackets. "Don't forget, tomorrow you'll miss algebra class."

As if Mickey Decker and a mysterious stranger were not enough to complicate my life, she had to remind me of the track meet. At the very thought my legs turned to Jell-O and butterflies ran hurdles in my stomach.

The all-city meet was the last one before the conference championship. To go on to conference, I had to place in at least one event, and that was not likely to happen. In one way it was a relief. Performing in front of a group of people terrified me. It had been Jane's idea to go out for track, not mine. "It'll be fun," she had promised.

The fun had not lasted longer than the first track meet when I came in last in the 220, and she had not done much better in the broad jump. It was embarrassing to realize that we were on the track team only through the generosity of Coach Thornton. I was too slow, and Jane was too awkward.

Jane immediately sensed my downcast mood at the mention of the meet. "Wendy, don't take it so seriously. So what if we're not athletes," she rationalized. "That's not nearly as important as trying."

I wasn't in the mood for one of her "Let's win one for the Gipper" speeches. "Don't start, Jane," I warned, but it was too late. I gritted my teeth and waited for her much rehearsed lecture.

"The fact that your mother's an artist, your dad's a writer/chef, and your sister is an absolute musical genius would intimidate anyone, but it doesn't give you the right to hide in a corner for the rest of your life. The only way to overcome shyness is to face it and fight it."

There was some kind of desperate logic to that, and I wanted to believe her. My mother had said the same thing. My dad insisted that he liked me just the way I was. Cammie (short for Camelia Rose), my nineteen-year-old sister and a piano prodigy, was less subtle. She just said, "Hang in there, Wendy."

At that point the bell sounded the beginning of first period. Like most school days, time passed slowly but surely. Inevitably sixth period came. As I entered room 212, my stomach churning, I reminded myself that God had given me the spirit of power and love. I prayed once more for guidance and courage to approach Mickey Decker.

A sense of calm and confidence came over me, and I was actually disappointed to see his desk empty. The whispered rumor around the room was that he had been suspended for swearing at a teacher, but I soon guessed the real reason was the distributed quiz papers Mr. Hardy had promised.

On the bus ride home, Jane was more subdued than usual, but as we reached our bus stop, she glanced nervously up and down the block. We both saw a flash of yellow at the end of the street.

In a whisper, her last words to me were, "Don't forget you promised to tell your father about that VW and the bald-headed man."

I hadn't forgotten that, but I had forgotten that we were having a guest for dinner.

Chapter Two

His name was Sean Richards.

Mom had told us about him the night before at our usual get-together before dinner in the family room. Several years ago when Mom opened the gallery, Dad was still teaching at the college, and Cammie and I were old enough to be doing our own thing, our mother got this brilliant idea for an old-fashioned family time every evening. We each talk about what we've done all day while we sip fruit or tomato juice. That part was Dad's idea. He said it was good for the digestive system.

"Good for the family," Mom said. Maybe it's because she never had any real family of her own that I know of. At least she never talks about them.

"Good way for Mom to have a captive audience," Cammie said. Mom really enjoyed talking about her work at the gallery. Her main purpose in opening it was to give young unrecognized artists a chance to exhibit their work.

Sean Richards was one of those. According to her he really had talent, and she was pretty pleased with herself for discovering him. Her eyes had sparkled as she explained.

"Of course, I didn't actually discover *him*. He kind

of found me . . . just walked into the shop with his portfolio. But it was a lucky break for both of us. He has such a technique with water color, and his pen and ink sketches are really excellent."

Then she had told us that she had invited Sean for dinner and would Dad please try to come up with something a little more traditional than what he usually serves us.

"Perhaps a chicken casserole, Rob," she had suggested, "and maybe a green salad."

Dad was agreeable. He's never refused my mother anything—except once. After she named Cammie "Camelia Rose," he put his foot down and said no other daughter of his was going to sound like a seed catalog advertisement. (I am grateful for this since Mom's next favorite flower is a petunia.)

Thinking about Dad brought a smile to my lips. I knew that when I opened the front door, the sound of his deep voice accompanied by his own electric orchestra—food processor, blender, and mixer—would greet me. He would be singing loudly and off-key his favorite song, "Polly Wolly Doodle." That's where my nickname, "Doodle Bug," comes from.

Tucked away in the music room upstairs, Cammie would be hard at work too. Even now, through the open window, the classical and harmonious strains of one of Beethoven's sonatas permeated the soft spring air.

Mom wouldn't be home yet. It's still kind of strange to think that she's off downtown running a business, and Dad is in the kitchen preparing dinner. Not to mention Cammie, who's preparing for an audition at the LeTour Conservatory of Music next month. That makes my family different from most, but special too.

Strolling up the long brick walk toward my front door, I was impressed again with the presence of spring everywhere, from the tall lilac bushes bordering the perimeter of the yard to the tiny grape hyacinths almost hidden in the shadow of the stately pine tree. I remembered the phrase Browning wrote, "God's in his heaven. All's right with the world."

That thought, coupled with the ordinary sights and sounds of my own home, dispelled the vague feelings of fear that had bothered me earlier. Jane did have an overactive imagination. Still, I had promised.

I found my father in the kitchen. His usual boisterous singing had subsided to a loud humming.

"Dad, have you got a minute to talk?"

"A little bit later, Doodle Bug, if it's not too urgent. This is the tricky part."

I watched in fascination as he diligently stirred some concoction in the top of a double boiler. With his other hand, he carefully sprinkled sparse portions of unknown herbs into the steamy mixture. Then leaning closely, he sniffed the subtle aroma. Apparently satisfied, he reduced the heat to a simmer and put a lid on the pot. Shoving his misted glasses up into the thatch of reddish brown hair, he turned to me.

"Maybe you could set the table while I finish up here?" he suggested.

A short time later, I brushed an imaginary wrinkle from the starched linen tablecloth on the dining room table and stepped back to admire my painstaking handiwork. The prisms of the fragile stemware collected rays from the late afternoon sun and threw them back in rainbows on the delicate china plates. Squinting at my upside down reflection in the bowl of a sterling silver teaspoon, I saw the image of my father standing behind me.

"OK, Wendy." The tiny lines around his green eyes crinkled as he smiled at my effort. "Nice," he said. "Now, what was it you wanted to talk about?"

But before I could open my mouth, the front door opened.

"Rob, Cammie, Wendy, we're here."

Mom had arrived with our guest.

"What did you think about Sean Richards?"

Since I had my mouth full of potato chips, I chewed and swallowed before answering Cammie. I sat in the middle of her bed with our survival kit spread out temptingly in front of me. She and I don't mean to be deliberately disloyal to Dad, but we keep a secret supply of goodies stashed in her room—potato chips, chocolate bars, cookies, and other things guaranteed to cause cavities and offset junk food withdrawal pains.

"Not what I expected," I replied.

Sean had been a surprise. In the first place, he couldn't have been but a couple of years older than Cammie.

Secondly, he was nicely dressed. I guess I had expected ragged jeans and a paint-smeared sweat shirt, scraggly hair or a scruffy beard. His gray wool slacks, burgundy tweed blazer, and pale blue shirt made him look like a bank executive.

Last, but not least, he was as handsome as a movie star with manners like a little kid on his best behavior.

"I thought he was OK," I added as I licked the middle of an Oreo cookie.

"Me, too, but I still don't know why Mom invited him here," Cammie said as she sat down at her dresser and began to brush her long black hair. "She's never done that with any of her young artists before."

"I don't know. Maybe she thinks he's really got a special talent or something," I suggested. "Maybe she just thought he looked hungry."

"Maybe. But didn't you notice the way she kept staring at him?"

"Mom? Stare? Never!"

"Discreetly, of course. Mom would never want to

make anyone feel uncomfortable. She's too much of a lady for that."

Cammie half-lowered her eyelids and glanced casually over her shoulder in an obvious imitation of our mother. With her classic oval face, dark brown eyes, and smooth olive complexion surrounded by abundant dark hair, Cammie was almost an exact replica of our Mom.

No such luck for me. I look too much like Dad, with limp reddish brown hair (Mom insists it's auburn) and fair skin that freckles or burns.

"Well, now that I think about it, I guess Mom did look at him strangely."

"Mysteriously," Cammie suggested in a dramatic whisper. "As though she were trying to remember something or trying to figure something out." She turned from the mirror, dropping the theatrical pose. "But did you also notice the way Sean kept watching her?"

I hated to admit that I was not as observant of other people as she was. "I guess so," I answered. "But she did look pretty tonight."

It was true. Mom was always pretty, but this evening she seemed to have taken extra pains. Her new mauve dress with a swirly skirt just kind of floated when she walked, and wearing her hair loose and lightly curled had made her look much younger.

"It wasn't just that," Cammie insisted. She was in the middle of her nightly exercise routine with her hands high over her head, counting rhythmically as she swept gracefully first to one side and then the other.

"One, two, three . . . it was more like . . . four, five, six. More like (change sides) . . . he knew something, something that we don't know."

I was intrigued. "What?"

Cammie stopped, both hands on her hips. "Honestly, Wendy, you are so naive sometimes, it's scary. How would I know?"

Dropping to the floor, she stretched her legs straight out in front of her, and, reaching to her toes with her hands, put her head down on her knees.

For my own benefit, I tried to sort out what Cammie had been talking about. "OK, Mom looked at Sean *questioningly*? And he looked at her *knowingly*?" We had studied adverbs in English. Mrs. Carroll would have been proud of me.

Cammie raised her head immediately. "Very good, Wendy. I couldn't have said it better myself."

"But it doesn't make any sense, Cammie," I argued. "What could he possibly know that we don't know? It's just your imagination."

"Or your lack of the same."

Twice in one day I had been accused of that.

"Didn't you think Sean looked awfully familiar?" Cammie stretched out on the floor and relaxed, but continued talking. I didn't know if she was talking to the ceiling, herself, or me.

"It was his smile . . . or his voice," she mused. The ceiling didn't answer, and I didn't either. Then she bolted upright and looked at me. "His eyes! That's it. I'm sure of it. I've seen those eyes before."

"Paul Newman," I responded quickly. "I noticed it right away."

Her look of scorn told me that was the wrong answer.

"You've probably seen him before, Cammie," I rationalized, "on the street or at the store."

"No, no. He's been here only a few days. He came to take some art seminar or something at the university. If I had seen him before, I would remember. Come on, Wendy, think. Didn't you notice it too?"

"Cammie, this is crazy. This whole conversation is crazy. Mom and Sean Richards looking at each other weird and his eyes . . ." But I had to admit there was something about Sean that intrigued me also. "Of course, you had more opportunity to look at his eyes than I did."

Cammie ignored my teasing. "They were deep blue and mysterious, and . . . and . . . I know I've seen him somewhere before, Wendy."

I shrugged. "It will probably come to you sooner or later."

"I guess. Anyway, I'm glad he's coming over again tomorrow."

Sean had been very complimentary about Dad's cooking and had even offered to do some illustrations for his new book. Dad had been delighted and he had invited Sean back the next day to discuss it further.

"I thought he was coming over to see Dad," I said.

"He is. But that doesn't mean I won't get to see him too. In fact, I intend to do just that. There's more to this situation than meets the eye. No pun intended."

"You've been reading too many romantic novels lately, Cammie."

"And you're too practical and down to earth to sense the mysteries of life, my prosaic little sister. Someday you've got to learn to rise above the ordinary, the everyday, and search out the deeper—"

She stopped in midsentence. "Now I remember! Come on." Cammie jumped up from the floor and grabbed my arm. The bag of cookies spilled across the yellow bedspread.

"Where are we going?"

"Sh-h-h," Cammie admonished as she carefully turned the knob of the bedroom door and peered out into the hall. "Sh, Mom and Dad are in their room. Don't make any noise," she warned as she cautiously stepped through the doorway and tiptoed toward the stairs.

Bravely I followed, wondering why it was necessary for us to sneak through our own house. Luckily, enough moonlight streamed through the windows to light our path. The downstairs looked eerie in the half darkness. The pale moonlight cast exaggerated shadows on the floor. My heart thumped loudly, and I held on to the stair rail for support. All I could do was follow Cammie's lead.

Hopefully she was headed toward the kitchen. I needed a glass of milk to wash down the last Oreo.

But she turned left at the bottom of the steps and proceeded past the door of the family room. Oh, well, I had guessed she hadn't come to watch TV.

"Ow!" I stumbled over a chair against the wall and let out a muffled cry of pain. Instantly Cammie turned and clamped her hand over my mouth.

"Sh-h-h!"

Heedless of the fact that she was suffocating me, she managed with her free hand to open the door to the studio and drag me inside. There she released me.

Gingerly I massaged my chin and cheeks with my fingertips and glared at Cammie. "What are we doing here?" I mouthed, afraid to speak, even in a whisper.

Cammie didn't answer, but she touched my shoulder and with her head motioned me over to the little storage room where Mom kept her canvases and paints and things.

Obediently I tagged behind her, being extra careful not to bump into anything else.

Once inside the smaller room, Cammie quietly closed the door, turned on the light, walked toward an easel in the middle of the floor, threw back the cloth covering it, and looked at me triumphantly.

I stared at the portrait. Staring back at me were deep blue, disturbingly familiar eyes.

"Well?" Cammie demanded. "Was I right?"

Chapter Three

I could only nod my head. The portrait of a young woman had been there for as long as I could remember. When Cammie and I were younger, we had sometimes come in here and looked at the painting, making up stories about the girl. They were mostly sad stories. I don't know why. She did not look sad. The blond hair framing the pale young face was like a halo. The beautiful, expressive eyes registered joy, not pain. Most of the picture was only sketched in airy brushstrokes, but the eyes were vivid and complete.

Cammie and I didn't say anything else. And after she had re-covered the portrait, we crept noiselessly back to her room. I was bursting with curiosity, but Cammie's excitement had changed to a pensive silence. I struggled to contain myself until after we had had our usual Bible reading and prayer time.

"It is just a coincidence, isn't it, Cammie?"

She shook her head in a thoughtful way. "I don't know, Wendy. I really don't know."

The same feeling of intrigue I had experienced earlier in the morning swept over me, and I remembered with guilt that I had said nothing to Dad. Yet, somehow, the mystery of a stranger in a yellow car paled in comparison to this.

After my own private bedtime prayers, I snuggled deep within my bed and tried to sleep. For a long time, visions of portraits, blue eyes, yellow VW's, and a bald-headed man prevented that.

It was almost enough to take my mind off the track meet.

Two hundred meters stretch endlessly ahead of me. The spectators in the stadium become a blur as I focus my attention only on circling the track. My legs ache. My muscles train to keep one foot following in precise rhythm after the other. My breath comes in short gasps. I hold my head high to suck in air. My heart pounds in sync with the plodding of my feet. I sprint, but it is too late. The other runners pass me by.

Dear Lord, let me finish. Don't let me quit now.

I slow my steps, gradually reducing the speed that propels my body. The muscles in my legs quiver, then respond to stillness.

"Wendy, are you listening to me?"

Louder than the noise of showers running, locker doors banging, and the chatter of thirty other girls, Jane's clear voice shattered the painful memory.

"Isn't it unbelievable, Wendy? I'm so excited I could die."

She towered over me, her dark brown curls untamed, her thin face flushed, and the silver braces on her teeth exposed in unashamed smile of triumph. Then without waiting for an answer, she skittered away like an awkward colt on legs too long for her body.

Grateful for a moment to myself, I watched her dance happily around the girls' locker room as she waited for her turn in the shower. My reprieve was only temporary.

"I finally did it," she announced. "Jane Olderfield,

class klutz! I showed them all right. How about you, Wendy? I didn't see all the final results. You did qualify for the conference meet, didn't you?"

She had to ask.

Still dressed in my dark blue track warm-ups, I slumped on the bench in front of the metal lockers. I mumbled something unintelligible as I picked at a stubborn knot in the laces of my shoe.

Jane was relentless. "I didn't hear what you said, Wendy."

"Uh, no, Jane, I didn't qualify," I admitted painfully.

"I'm sorry, Wendy. I naturally assumed that if *I* made it, you would. Conference track meet, here I come. *And* . . . guess what?"

I couldn't guess.

"*You-know-who* even congratulated me!"

Since Jane talks not only with her mouth but her face, her hands, and anything else available, she emphasized the *you-know-who* with raised eyebrows, a knowing smile, and a twist of her head as she turned and groped her way toward the shower. Without her glasses, it was a fifty/fifty chance she would find it.

She was no more in the dark than I was. *You-know-who* could be anybody, though I was reasonably sure it was a boy.

The dressing room was quieter now, but steamy. It smelled like sweaty sneakers and disinfectant. I felt clammy and sick to my stomach. Most of the other girls had showered, dressed, and left, but I still sat on the bench as Jane came out of the shower. She grabbed for her towel, then fumbled for her glasses.

"Maybe you didn't *try* hard enough," she announced, struggling to pull a pink T-shirt down over her still wet shoulders. "Or maybe it was just my lucky day. You-know-what-I-mean?" Once again the raised eyebrows and cryptic smile.

I shrugged. Jane thinks I can decipher everything she says even when she speaks in code, which she uses whenever we're around other people so they won't know what we're talking about.

It works well. I don't know either most of the time.

At this point, I didn't even try. I just didn't feel like playing guessing games. Anyway, with Jane sometimes it's safer not to know. I had a feeling today was one of those times.

"Feeling sorry for yourself again?" she asked, but she didn't give me time to answer. "It's the old *last one chosen for the team at recess* syndrome, you know. You just can't forgive Patsy McDonald, can you?"

I looked up in exasperation. "Patsy McDonald? What does Patsy McDonald have to do with anything?"

"Don't play dumb. I know you haven't forgotten. In fifth grade, she was always the first one picked for the team, and you were always picked last."

"*You* and I were always picked last," I reminded her bitterly.

She ignored me. "Let's face it, Wendy. You can't help it that you're not athletic. It's not your fault that you're so uncoordinated."

I struggled for self-control and lost. "Me?" I shrieked. "I'm not the one who's been rushed to the emergency room so many times for X-rays and stitches that they named the new wing the Olderfield Orthopedic Center."

"For my grandfather," she responded icily. "You know he raised the money. Besides my mother tends to panic."

I could understand why. I glared at Jane, but she went right ahead, throwing clothes into her gym bag and psychoanalyzing me at the same time.

"After all, Wendy, in the general scheme of life, running faster than someone else is just not that important.

It's nothing to be ashamed of either. Just remember, *someone* had to be last."

Who could argue with logic like that? Who would want to? I didn't even try.

"If you don't hurry, you're going to miss the activities bus, and we'll have to walk home," Jane said as she stood in front of the mirror combing her damp curls, seemingly oblivious to my pouting.

"You go ahead," I insisted. "There's no reason for both of us to walk. I haven't showered yet."

She didn't protest. "OK. I hope *you-know-who* is on the bus. Maybe we can get off at the Burger Barn for a *you-know-what*."

I was still in the *you-know-where*, but I nodded at her as if it all made sense.

She started toward the door, but couldn't resist one parting shot. I cringed as she turned back to me, but she was kind.

"I am sorry, Wendy, and remember, 'God don't make no junk.' "

I smiled. "Thanks, Jane." I knew that. It was the one thing that kept me going. He must have a purpose for me.

There was no hot water left in the showers, so I decided to go home as I was. I hoped I had missed the bus. I didn't want to face anybody right now. Walking the two miles home alone would clear my mind. Brooding about the track meet was pointless, and I determined to forget all about it.

I headed for home in the direction of Crescent Heights, the small subdivision a short way from the high school. It wasn't the most appealing way to go, but it was the shortest.

Crescent Heights sounds like it should be a romantic Gothic estate in an English countryside or something out of an Agatha Christie novel. It's not. Why it has that name is anybody's guess. It was probably named that to disguise what it really is—a low rental housing project.

All of the small wooden frame houses are alike: long narrow duplexes set on concrete slabs with no porches. Most are in need of paint. Age and use have defeated, not mellowed, them.

The sameness of the worn, shabby houses depressed me. Crowded close together as they were, there was very little space left over for lawns. Mostly it was hard-packed earth. Spring, which was so evident elsewhere in town, had passed Crescent Heights by. Time had passed it by. I shivered thinking about it.

Maybe it was because I already felt so down that this place got to me. Maybe I identified with it because it was so ordinary, and today I felt the same way. I don't know. I only know I felt sad for the poor little houses and bare lawns.

I felt sorry, too, for the people who lived there.

I couldn't help but wonder if God loves some of us more than others because the houses in my neighborhood were so very different. Our own home, built from Mom's plans, boasted a large daylight studio for her, a modern kitchen for Dad, and an acoustically correct music room large enough for Cammie's grand piano.

Maybe if we lived in one of those small houses in Crescent Heights, Mom and Dad and Cammie wouldn't be so talented. It must be easier for people who don't have to worry about money to put their time and energy into things like art and music and books.

We weren't rich, I supposed, but we were well off. Dad's first book had done all right, and, even though he was on a leave of absence from the college, he still drew a salary. Even Mom's art gallery was finally beginning to show a profit.

Thinking of my own family, my home, and my neighborhood made me feel like an intruder in Crescent

Heights. I walked faster and came to the corner of the block. I didn't belong here.

At the end of the street was a large empty space, about two acres of rough ground. The sparse grass was brown and brittle. Trash and empty pop cans and bottles littered the area. Except for its similar look of neglect, this open spot seemed out of place among the closely situated houses. It was as though it had been left there by mistake.

Some young mothers were watching small children playing in a dirt pile. On a splintery bench with peeling paint sat two old people. A group of kids kicked a soccer ball around. One of these boys was Mickey Decker.

I guess I tried too hard not to stare at him or the soccer game. The next thing I knew, something tore into the pit of my stomach and took away both my breath and my feet. I landed squarely on my *you-know-what* in the dirt, holding firmly to a black and white object.

Before I could catch my breath, a hand grabbed my arm, hauling me roughly to my feet, and an angry voice demanded, "Why don't you look where you're going?"

Flushed with embarrassment, I stood there clinging to the ball and staring into dark flashing eyes.

"Hi, Mickey," I gasped.

"Wendy Thomsen? What're you doing here?"

"Playing soccer?" I asked with a nervous giggle.

"Sorry," he mumbled apologetically.

"That's OK. I should have paid more attention to where I was going."

"You been at the track meet?"

I nodded. That should have been obvious. There had to be some good reason why I was dressed in baggy sweats with my red hair straggling out of the pony-tail clip. My freckles were probably lit up like Christmas lights.

"What're you doing here?" he repeated. "You miss

the bus? You don't live around here, do you?"

"I missed the bus," I admitted. "Do you live around here?" It was a dumb question, but our previous conversations had been limited to our mutual distrust for the x's and y's in algebra class. And it postponed the real question I should be asking.

"Yeah," he answered. "Down the street." He nodded in the direction from which I had come.

Just then one of the other kids yelled at him, "Hey, Mick, you gonna play or what?"

He shrugged and flashed me a smile. Then he held out his hands for the ball, which I was still hanging on to. I realized we had reached the far edge of the park. It was now or never.

"Mickey, I . . . we . . . I . . ." Through a mouth as dry as sand, my voice came out in a sad squeak.

He eyed me quizzically. Then I recalled the spirit of power and love, and as I extended the ball to him, I spoke again. This time the words came with a clarity and boldness that surprised me.

"The youth group at our church is having a fellowship to celebrate the last day of school. We'd like you to come."

He stared at me. "Do what?" he asked, with undisguised disbelief in his voice and eyes. "A fellowship? Is that like where you sit around and drink Kool-Aid and eat cookies and listen to some old guy preach?"

I swallowed hard and plunged in. "Not exactly. We were planning something more like a cook-out and swimming and games. You already know some of the kids in the group and . . ." My words died to a whisper as he interrupted.

"Me?" he asked with disdain. "You want me to come to a church party?"

I nodded.

He snickered. "Well, that might be good for a laugh

at that. Mickey Decker at a church party. I thought that was just for the good guys."

The implied ridicule almost made me angry, but then he added, "I'll tell you what, Wendy Thomsen. I'll think it over. Yeah, that's what I'll do. I'll think it over."

He took the soccer ball and glanced hastily over his shoulder at his waiting teammates. Then he smiled. The brittle quality of his voice had faded when he said quietly, "Thanks, Wendy. No one's ever invited me to a church fellowship before."

He tucked the soccer ball securely under his arm and sauntered casually back to the game.

Chapter Four

For a moment I stayed and watched as Mickey placed a well-aimed kick that resumed the play of the game. Gone was my frustration with the track meet; gone was my irritation with Jane. Only a sense of peace remained and the joy that comes from allowing God to control a situation. I hoped I would remember that in the future.

Thank you, Lord, for replacing my timidity with your power, I prayed.

Jane had been right. I didn't really know Mickey Decker. The unmistakable sincerity of his last words had allowed me a glimpse into a different Mickey than the one my imagination had preconceived.

I can't say that I flew home, but I surely don't remember my feet touching the ground. If only I could run that 220 now!

The quietness of our house surprised me. The usual electric whir from the kitchen was absent. There was silence, too, from the upstairs music room.

I could not remember the last time that Cammie had missed practice. And why wasn't Dad getting dinner ready? Was it possible that he had flipped and planned to take us out for pizza? Even in my ecstatic condition, I knew this was pure fantasy. Then I heard Cammie's voice in the kitchen of all places.

This in itself was totally out of the ordinary. Cammie never went near the kitchen unless it was her turn to do dishes. I think she's allergic to any kind of domestic activity like cooking. I knew she was too smart to go to the kitchen for a snack. Only a rabbit would be dumb enough to do that. Even the baking soda in our refrigerator gets bored. Perhaps she was just visiting with Dad.

But it was Sean Richards and my sister that I found sitting at the glass-topped kitchen table. Cammie was turned in profile to me, her small even nose and chin silhouetted in the sunshine. She looked stiff, like she had a crick in her neck. Then I realized she was posing. On a sketch pad in front of him, Sean was drawing a picture of her with short, sure strokes. Dad was nowhere in sight.

"Hi," I said, self-consciously announcing my presence. I stood at the kitchen entrance, not sure if I should go in or wait for an invitation. "Thirsty," I mumbled and headed toward the sink for water.

"Oh, hi, Wendy. Come on in. Dad had to go out to the store for something he forgot." Cammie didn't move her head as she explained, but she did glance sideways at Sean. "I was keeping Sean company until Dad got back. You hadn't forgotten that Sean was coming over?"

He stopped long enough to acknowledge my presence with a tilt of his pencil.

Between swallows of water, I nodded and tried to smile. The whole scene was wrong. In the first place, Dad is a totally organized shopper. It isn't like him at all to suddenly remember something he needs from the store. That's part of his program for healthy cooking: plan ahead, make a list, and refrain from impulse shopping.

In the second place, Cammie doesn't usually allow fire, flood, or famine to interrupt her practice time. Certainly not just being gracious. Besides, she had a strange expression on her face that was vaguely familiar. Where had I seen it before? Then I remembered. Last night! It was exactly the same way Mom had looked at Sean across the dinner table. Staring, but not staring; knowing, but not knowing. Being with Mickey had erased from my memory everything that had happened last night, the escapade in the dark and Cammie's obsession with Sean's eyes. It was true enough. Those deep blue eyes, that pale blond coloring, even his long slender fingers looked so much like the lady's in the portrait. So much, that it was almost scary.

In a gentlemanly fashion, Sean rose from his chair. "Why don't you join us, Wendy?" he asked politely. "I was trying my hand at a sketch of your sister." He looked at her and smiled. "She's a good model, but now it's your turn. How about it?"

I was flattered, but before I had a chance to say anything, Cammie answered for me. "No, Sean, Wendy always gets right to her homework as soon as she gets home from school. Exams are coming up. Right Wendy? Besides, I want you to see Mom's studio."

"Uh . . ." I fumbled for words. *Me*? *Homework*? Then Cammie looked straight at me, and her dark eyes relayed a message I could not mistake. "Oh, sure, yes, I do. Homework. Exams."

I turned and fled from the kitchen. Even *I* was smart enough to understand that Cammie wanted me out.

The doorbell rang, and I hurried toward the front of the house. In the dimness of the hallway to the foyer, daylight streaming through the skinny windows of the door made bright patches on the polished tile floor. I hopscotched my way from one elongated rectangle to the next toward the entrance, fully expecting Jane to be on the other side of the door.

Coming to gloat over her victory at the track meet, I

thought. Oh, well, I could handle that. She was entitled.

Still, when did Jane ever ring the bell? Usually she just burst in like one of the family.

With my hand on the doorknob, I glanced through one of the narrow windows, blinked hard, and looked again. Where *was* Jane when I needed her? No one was in sight, but parked right in front of our house was the infamous yellow Volkswagen!

Jerking open the door, I stood face-to-face with a man.

"Mrs. Thomsen?" he inquired.

I dragged my gaze from the automobile to the squat little man wearing a hat and dark pin-striped suit with shiny creases.

"Are you Mrs. Thomsen?" he repeated.

"No, that's my mother." Then, wide-eyed, I watched him remove the gray felt hat and mop his perspiring brow. A fringe of shaggy hair bisected his head midway between prominent ears and the top of his shiny scalp. For one moment of shocked silence, my mind refused to accept what my eyes saw. Then before I could stop myself, the exclamation leapt from my mouth.

"You're . . . you're bald-headed!"

Immediately I clapped my hand over my mouth to stifle my outcry and felt my cheeks burn with embarrassment.

His own weathered complexion colored a deeper shade also as he speedily re-covered his head. A quick frown knit his bushy eyebrows together in a straight line, and he peered at me intently with small eyes of an undistinguishable color.

"Perhaps this is a bad time?" he asked.

"Y-yes—n-no—," I stuttered, clinging tightly to the door frame. "For what? A bad time for what?"

"Allow me to introduce myself." He squared his shoulders. "My name is Carter Crenshaw. I am a real estate agent, and I have some prospective buyers for this house."

"For this house?" I asked, thoroughly confused.

"I realize that this residence is not for sale at the moment," he hastily explained. "But my clients are desirous of purchasing in this neighborhood. We thought that perhaps if the price were right, you would consider the sale."

"I'm sorry, but I'm really not the one you need to talk with."

"Then, perhaps you would be so good as to call one of your parents to the door?"

"I can't do that," I answered. "I mean, both Mom and Dad are out."

He grinned slightly, the beady eyes opened wider, and his eyebrows relaxed to their proper position.

"Then perhaps you would grant me the privilege of viewing the inside of the house so that I could at least share that information with my clients?" He shifted his stance from one foot to the other and peered past me into the foyer.

I quickly considered the idea. He seemed harmless enough, though somewhat pretentious. It might be fun to show off the house, but second thoughts convinced me not to.

"I'm sorry, Mr.—er—"

"Crenshaw."

"I don't think I should do that, either, without my parents here," I contended.

This time clear disappointment registered in his face. "Well, I understand that. I respect your reticence to allow a perfect stranger into your home. Maybe you could just tell me something about the home? It may not interest my buyers at all. They have some particular ideas about what they are looking for. The lady fancies herself a sculptor."

"A sculptor? Then she'd probably love my mother's studio," I suggested proudly.

"Studio? That's interesting," he said with a touch of indifference. "How many baths?"

"Three."

He took a small pad from his inside jacket pocket and jotted notes as I answered questions.

"A separate dining room, I suppose?"

I nodded.

"And bedrooms?"

"Of course," I giggled.

"No, I mean, how many? And where did you say the studio was located?"

"Four bedrooms, and I didn't say, but it's at the north back corner of the house. Right below my bedroom," I added.

"Oh, I see, on the ground floor then. That's good."

He replaced the pad and pencil in his pocket.

"But don't you want to know about the kitchen or music room—?"

He stopped me with a raised hand. "No, you've been more than helpful already. I won't take any more of your time. Please tell your parents that I called and I will definitely contact them another time. Crenshaw," he said. "Carter Crenshaw. You won't forget?"

I watched as he strutted toward the car. He paused as he opened the door, then tipped his hat to me before settling himself behind the steering wheel.

I was not the only one who saw this gesture. Cammie and Sean had come from the direction of the studio. Sean stared through the open doorway, seemingly amused by the spectacle.

"Who was that man, Wendy?" he questioned as we watched the car drive away.

"Just a real estate agent," I replied without going into details. "Why?"

"Oh, nothing. For a moment, I thought that I knew him. Only my imagination, I guess," he said to Cammie as they started down the front walk.

I turned from the door with an *I told you so* chuckle. I couldn't wait to see Jane.

"Thief masquerading as a detective," I mimicked under my breath and took the stairs two at a time toward my room. I was eager to talk to Cammie about Sean, but right now, a hot shower topped my priority list. First I deposited my worn track shoes in the trash can. "Rest in peace," I mumbled, turning away with no hesitation or regret.

When I finished in the shower, I could hear Dad in the kitchen and Cammie practicing furiously in the music room. My curiosity would have to wait. In the meantime, I blow-dried my hair and slipped into clean jeans and a pink cotton sweater.

"Rob, Cammie, Wendy," rang through the house. Mom was home. A glance in the mirror assured me that my freckles were now subdued and my straggly hair had been brushed into a fiery gleam. I was ready for family time.

A few minutes later, I watched as Mom settled herself in her usual place on the sofa, and Cammie plopped comfortably onto the multi-colored braid rug on the floor. I chose the big leather recliner, while Dad passed out glasses of chilled freshly squeezed orange juice. Looking from one to the other of their faces sent a little shiver of love through me and silently I offered a short prayer of thanksgiving for these special ones, my family.

At last I would have a chance to keep my promise to Jane and tell Dad about the lemon-colored car and the bald-headed man—but not yet. We had a kind of ritual to this.

Mom first. I tried to focus my attention on her recital of how she had finally closed a deal on a painting. She had been negotiating this for several weeks.

Then Dad. He had an amusing story about some lady in the supermarket with three small children who kept putting things into her basket faster than she could put them back on the shelf. It was funny the way he told it.

Cammie was next. Until now she had sat still and quiet, but there was a mischievous glint in her eye as she announced that she had a date with Sean for Friday evening.

I was surprised at Mom's reaction. She sat silently, but her fingers nervously twisted the long strand of creamy pearls that lay against her white silk blouse.

"I didn't know you knew him that well, Cammie," she said at last.

Before my sister could answer, Dad explained, "Joanna, Sean came over today to talk to me about the sketches for the book. Cammie offered to entertain him while I was at the market."

If Mom questioned this, she didn't let on. She knew as well as I that there was something strange about the whole story.

"That's right, Mom. I thought Sean might be interested in some of your work so I gave him a tour of your studio," Cammie said innocently.

Mom suddenly jerked forward like a puppet on a string. "My studio?" She gripped the arm of the couch and stared wide-eyed at Cammie.

"I thought he would enjoy it, and I was right. He was impressed with all of your things, but he especially liked that old painting in the storage room."

"You showed the . . . portrait . . . to Sean?" Mom's voice died away to a choked whisper, and her face paled.

Looking at her reminded me of a poem I read once. The poem, by Emily Dickinson, began, "I like a look of agony, because I know it's true. . . ."

I had never quite understood until that moment just what she meant by that, but now I knew. On my mother's face was the look of genuine agony. But what I couldn't understand was, why?

The expression faded as quickly as it had come, and she regained her composure almost immediately.

Cammie threw a worried glance at me as she nodded. "Is there something wrong with that? It's my favorite portrait."

Mom shook her head. "I suppose not," she murmured.

I looked at my sister. The mischievous look had been replaced with one of guilty regret. Surely she had not expected such a response from our mother.

Now it was my turn. I had so much to tell. I thought of the track meet, but that was past history. Then there was Mickey, but hunger pangs in my stomach forced a quick decision.

"Dad, are you planning to sell this house?" I asked abruptly.

"Of course not, Wendy," he answered immediately. "Why do you ask?"

Then I launched into my tale beginning with Jane and ending with, "He said to tell you he would be back."

"How strange," Mom commented. "Did he tell you his name?"

I sighed. "Several times. Carter Crenshaw," I pronounced carefully.

Mom's back stiffened. She sat straight up, away from the sofa cushion.

"Carter Crenshaw?" she repeated in a gasp and met Dad's swift glance. "Are you sure?"

I hesitated, startled again by the look on her face. "I think so. Yes, Carter Crenshaw," I said again.

"Do you know him, Mom?" Cammie asked.

She shook her head quickly. "No, no, of course not.

It's just such an unusual name."

"There's something else strange too," Cammie added. "Sean saw him and thought he recognized him."

Mom's gaze shifted rapidly from Cammie and then to Dad. A moment of silence passed. During that moment it seemed like the sunlight had suddenly changed to night. Dad stood and gallantly offered Mom his arm.

"I think it's time for dinner, Joanna."

Her features changed from a frozen stare, and she nodded, "Yes, Rob."

Cammie held me back as we started toward the dining room and whispered, "What have I done, Wendy? I feel awful. I never expected anything like that."

I felt the same way. Carter Crenshaw was certainly not an ordinary name, but, for some reason, Mom knew more than she was saying. It had frightened her.

And that frightened me.

Chapter Five

I went to bed that night with a queasy feeling in the pit of my stomach. I tried to convince myself that I had overdosed on Twinkies, but it was the image of my mother's stricken face that haunted my dreams.

In spite of that, the next morning I looked forward to my algebra class for the first time. It wouldn't be until last period, and, in the meantime, I had to endure English, which is one thing I can take or leave. The literature part is OK. Unlike most of the other kids, I really dig poetry. But today was "Journal Day."

I don't know who ever thought up the idea of writing in a journal. Keeping a private diary at home—locked up and hidden under my socks—is one thing, but having to write something in a journal at school for a teacher to read is something else altogether. But twice a week we were required to do just that.

I had planned to write something about Mickey in my journal today, but what I had planned and what I wrote were two different things. I was going to say something about meeting him in the park and how it made me feel. Instead I wrote,

"Jane Olderfield used to be my best friend, but no more!"

Because of an early dental appointment, Jane had not been on the bus, but I had met her in the school cafeteria for lunch as usual. I always walk a respectful distance behind Jane just for insurance. In case she trips and drops her lunch tray, I can look in the opposite direction and pretend I have never seen her before in my life. Seriously, she's only done this once or twice and today was one of her lucky days because she got all the way to a table without even spilling a drop of milk.

Most kids moan and groan about the food in the cafeteria, but to me it's like a bit of heaven. Just the smell makes my mouth water. In the fast food line where I always go, I can get greasy tacos and even greasier french fries and other delicacies we're never allowed at home. Dad thinks the school lunches are well-rounded, nutritious and according to the standards of the Department of Health. Oh, well . . . his ignorance is my bliss.

I was busily shoveling in the french fries just like I hadn't eaten in a week when Jane went into this weird contortion. She jerked her head sideways toward the door and rolled her eyes clockwise at the same time. Maybe Dad was right. Maybe this kind of food did poison our systems. Muffled through the napkin she held over her mouth, she was speaking some kind of foreign language that I couldn't understand. It sounded like someone talking to a dentist with a mouth full of hardware.

Reluctantly, I put down my french fry and stared in the direction of her spastic head movement. Her eyes became as wide as saucers then, and she threw her napkin down in disgust.

"I told you *not* to look," she hissed through clenched teeth.

"How did I know what you were saying? I thought maybe there was bug spray in our hamburger. Anyway, what is it that I was not supposed to look at?" I asked, desperately scanning the entire cafeteria.

With a sigh of contempt, Jane covered her eyes with her hand, propped her elbow up on the table barely missing her lunch tray, and shook her head ruefully.

Still without moving her mouth, she said, "*You-know-who* just walked into the cafeteria."

I didn't want to alarm her or cause her to go into a relapse, so I looked down at my plate and without moving my head tried once again to look around the room and decide which of the 150 possibilities Jane's *you-know-who* could be.

She continued to speak through her meshed braces. "Is he coming this way?"

I hadn't a clue.

"Is *who* coming this way?" I was hopeless to figure it out on my own. I found myself following her lead and talking out of the side of my mouth, looking around, but without moving my head. Whatever she had must be contagious. My french fries were getting colder and greasier by the second.

"I hate to be so blunt, but WHO are we not looking at?" I begged.

"Russell Brown," she whispered finally.

My hand stopped midway between plate and mouth—catsup dripping from my now-cold french fry. I stared at her incredulously. Surely I had misunderstood what she said.

"Russell Brown?" I repeated. And then hastily, "Oh, hi, Russell," as he walked over to our table, tray in hand, and made motions as if he wanted to sit down with us.

Russell meticulously unfolded his paper napkin and placed it in his lap, and opened his carton of milk. He had the standard school lunch: meatloaf, string beans, canned peaches, and a slice of whole wheat bread. The guilt I felt about my taco and french fries was easy to rationalize away after looking at him—meatloaf and string beans certainly hadn't done him much good.

Don't get me wrong. There was nothing terrible about Russell if you like short, dull, and baby-faced fellows. On tiptoes he came only within reach of Jane's shoulders, and his myopic eyes were hidden behind glasses almost as thick as hers. He had to keep pushing them up on his nose everytime he said anything. Obviously Jane was entranced, but I couldn't decide if the look on her face reflected the thrill of victory or the agony of defeat.

What happened next can be summed up in only one word—*catastrophe!*

The tables in the lunchroom are like picnic tables with the seats attached to the sides, so the only way to exit them is either to straddle the seat with one leg or to shimmy out sideways. Neither of these maneuvers can be achieved gracefully.

With Jane on one side of me and *you-know-who* on the other, I decided to try the straddle method. So there I stood with one foot still planted firmly under the table and the other one on the outside of the bench—my tray balanced precariously on both hands—when Jane dropped her purse.

She reached under the table to retrieve it, bumped my leg and, of course, came up right under my tray. It sounds like a scene from an old "I Love Lucy" re-run, but it's the truth. Jane's rising head hit the tray just as my foot slipped, and I plunged to the floor.

With one leg still draped over the bench, the other sprawled out in front of me, and the remains of taco, lettuce and tomato in my hair and on my face and clothes, I sat on the floor and glared at Jane with malice in my heart.

"Really, Wendy, you should be more careful," she admonished innocently, stifling a giggle. "You're getting to be almost as clumsy as I am."

My thoughts at that moment were so far from being Christian that I gritted my teeth and counted to ten. But before I had a chance to come up with some adequately icy response, two hands reached down to me, one grasping my elbow and the other my tray, and hauled me from the floor.

This could happen twice in the same lifetime only to me! Mickey Decker grinned as he casually flicked a piece of lettuce from my hair.

"You all right?" he asked.

"Sure," I replied lamely, brushing taco shell crumbs from my shirt and scraping a piece of tomato that matched the color of my face from my sleeve. "Thanks."

He smiled. "It's OK. See you in algebra."

Watching him stroll away, I wished I could crawl under the table and never come out again.

"No smile today, Wendy? When did you get so serious about algebra?"

Either Mickey had forgotten all about my falling at his feet, or he was being kind. Either way, I was grateful. For once my unsmiling expression had nothing to do with algebra.

I was sulking.

Memories of today's fiasco were still fresh, too fresh. And I hadn't even had a chance to tell Jane that her so-called thief had changed into a harmless real estate agent. Then, of course, even though she'll probably fall flat on her face, Jane was on the conference track meet team while I was not. I guess I was just a little angry—with some jealousy thrown in for good measure. I knew that was not a Christian attitude.

Well, anyway, that's why I wasn't smiling, but it's impossible not to smile back at someone as cute as Mickey. I looked into those black eyes, took a deep breath, and tried to be nonchalant.

"Oh, I was just trying to finish my homework. These last two problems really gave me trouble."

He stood right by my desk. I couldn't avoid staring at his muscles. Then I remembered the cafeteria again and I guess I blushed. At least my face felt strangely warm.

"Yeah, me too," he admitted. "What answers did you get?"

I willingly handed him my homework as he sat down at his own desk and opened his notebook. As he took the paper, he smiled at me again. I almost wished he wouldn't do that. It just kind of melted me inside. Maybe all that junk food was finally turning my brain to mush.

"Same answers, so we're either both right or both wrong," he said, returning the assignment to me.

We were probably both wrong, but who cared?

Mickey turned around as the tardy bell rang. I had sat behind him most of the year, but I had never noticed before how small his ears were or how his hair curled softly on his neck.

Algebra is the last class of the day, and I was considering whom I would sit by on the bus (since Jane would probably be with Russell Brown) when Mickey surprised me by asking if I was going to walk home.

I never walked home except when I missed the bus for some reason like the day of the track meet, but I thought, *Why not*? Especially if his question also included an invitation.

"I thought maybe I could walk with you," he offered. "At least part way."

"Uh . . . OK," I answered coolly, gathering up my books in my arms. "I get tired of riding that stupid bus. It's so noisy and crowded. Really I prefer to walk home."

"That's funny," Mickey said, giving me a quizzical look. "I've never seen you before the day of the track meet, but maybe you usually go the other way."

"Yeah, that's right," I agreed hastily. "I usually go the other way."

It didn't take us long to walk across the high school campus and start down the street toward the forlorn little park. Sparkling and witty conversation was not my thing, but it didn't seem necessary with Mickey. I knew I should have said something more about the Project Outreach fellowship, but I let my shyness take over and walked silently beside him.

In southeast Idaho, spring usually runs a zigzag course—one day an anticipation of summer and the next a remembrance of winter; but today was just what a spring day should be—warm, sunny and wonderful.

We stopped at the edge of the park. Mothers were there with their small children and some boys were playing ball just as they had been the first time.

"Want to sit down for a minute?" Mickey asked, motioning toward the weatherbeaten bench, which was empty today.

I nodded.

After we sat down, I looked around and then said, "I didn't realize until yesterday that there was a park here. Does it have a name?"

"Nah. It's not a park at all. Anyway, it doesn't matter because it won't be here much longer."

"Why not?" I asked in surprise. Mickey sounded sad or maybe resentful. I couldn't tell.

"Have you noticed how Fourth Street kind of curves around here? It makes a slight jog. Well, the big guys at city hall think that traffic will flow more easily if they straighten out the street or something. They'll have to cut straight through the edge of these vacant lots. So, bye-bye park."

"Don't you have the right to say anything about it?"

"Me?" Mickey sounded contemptuous.

"Not just you, but everyone who lives around here and uses the park."

He laughed. "It doesn't belong to us. Nobody asked our opinion. I just talked to some surveyors who were messing around here last week."

"But where will the kids in the neighborhood play?"

He shrugged. "Who knows? In the street maybe. They'll manage. We learn young to be survivors."

That sounded strange to me. I had no idea what he meant. He seemed angry and proud at the same time.

"Survivors?" I questioned. "What do you mean?"

"You wouldn't understand," Mickey replied with undisguised bitterness in his voice. "Your family has plenty of money and everything else. You don't have to worry about the next meal or how to feed one more baby or what to do if your social security or welfare is late and you can't pay the rent on time."

He spoke of things unknown to me. If he was trying to make me feel guilty, he had succeeded. We weren't rich, but he was right—we had never had to worry about things like that. Suddenly my life seemed too easy and comfortable. There are worse problems in the world than not making a track team or being hurt by your best friend.

"I'm sorry, Mickey, I didn't think . . . Surely there's something—"

He interrupted me. "Forget it. It's not your problem. Who cares anyway?"

Abruptly his mood changed. "Hey, I didn't ask you to walk home with me so I could cry on your shoulder. Let's keep walking over to Marty's Market and get a Coke."

Marty's Market, at the end of the street, had a couple of booths. We sat on cracked red vinyl seats and drank Cherry Cokes. Mickey looked across at me and smiled.

"Sorry if I unloaded on you," he apologized. "Sometimes I get kind of down, and it's nice to talk to someone."

He reached across the table and put his hand on mine very gently.

"Hey, I like the way you do that," he teased.

"Do what?" I asked. My heart was thumping.

"Blush." He grinned. "You did it today in the cafeteria . . ."

I groaned.

" . . . and yesterday in the park," he continued relentlessly.

"About yesterday," I began timidly. "You do remember about the fellowship?"

He eyed me cautiously.

"You said you'd think about it." The words rushed out.

"Yeah, I thought about it, and . . ." He moved his hand away from mine and stirred the ice in his glass with his straw. "And I'll go to your church party on one condition."

Chapter Six

"Me?" I cried in response to Mickey's startling proposal. "You want to go out with me?"

"That's what I said." He bent his straw in half, stuck it in the empty glass, and looked at me. Then he repeated his offer. "If you'll go out with me tomorrow night, then I'll come to your fellowship thing."

It sounded like a dare. My heart pounded, and my hands felt icier than the slippery glass they squeezed. Could I? Should I say yes? But he didn't give me time to think.

"I don't know why I've waited so long to ask you. I guess I was scared."

Mickey Decker? THE Mickey Decker? Scared?

"Of what?" I asked, unbelieving.

He shrugged. "You know. I'm from Crescent Heights. We don't exactly run in the same territory. Everyone knows about your family."

I sighed. "I'm the ordinary one, Mickey."

He looked straight at me. His voice rang with sincerity. "You're not ordinary to me."

The words echoed and re-echoed in my mind as I hurried home. And I knew it was true. Not in the way he meant it. Someday I would be able to explain to him that in God's eyes, no one is ordinary. But later. It was a lesson I was only beginning to learn.

I thought I would explode with excitement as I danced up the walk to our front door. Mom's car wasn't in the drive yet. That was good, because there was something I wanted to do.

I bypassed the kitchen, hurried to my own room where I could be alone, and knelt by my bed. It felt funny, and I remembered that I hadn't done it in a long time, not since Mom used to tuck us in with, "Now I lay me down to sleep."

"Thank you, Lord," I prayed. Jubilation, welling up in me, filled my throat and stopped my voice. I started again. "Thank you, Lord, for giving me the courage to invite Mickey to the party, and for giving him the courage to accept."

I realized that it had taken courage, though in a different way.

"And—it's nice about the date too," I added hastily.

I scrunched my eyes tighter and tried to visualize Mickey. But all I could recall was his warm smile and the soft touch of his hand on mine. That's when I understood that the good looks weren't nearly as important as the fact that being with him made me feel special.

Maybe that's what Jane saw in Russell Brown. Maybe he made her feel special. Being short and nearsighted didn't matter. I was instantly ashamed of the bad feelings I had been harboring.

"And, Lord," I whispered. "Please forgive me for being angry with Jane."

Now I felt better. Right after dinner, I would go over and apologize to her.

But first there was family discussion, and I couldn't wait to share my good news with Cammie, Mom, and Dad. I also wanted to ask my father about the little park in Crescent Heights. Mickey had said no one cared, but, for some reason, I did. If there was any way to stop its destruction, Dad would know.

Lured both by fragrant cinnamon smells and hoping to speed Dad along, I headed for the kitchen.

With his shirt sleeves rolled above his elbows, he was rolling out some thin pastry dough. Then with care he lifted it and draped it neatly in a pie plate.

"Apple pie," he announced proudly.

I must have looked surprised because he began to explain.

"Even I get hungry for something sweet and gooey sometimes, Wendy," he confessed with a chuckle, sticking a slice of the tangy apple into my open mouth.

Between succulent crunches, I had to laugh. He was like a little boy caught with his hands in the cooky jar.

"Besides," he added, "I thought we all deserved a treat."

"Is Mom home yet?" Cammie asked, walking into the kitchen.

Dad slid the pie into the oven and adjusted the timer before he answered. "She phoned a few minutes ago. She's going to be late, something about a client and a late appointment."

"Dad, do you think Mom is working too hard lately?" Cammie asked suddenly.

He rubbed his floury hands on his apron and shook his head. "She always works too hard, Cammie. You know that." But he looked at her uncertainly and worry lines creased his brow.

"But she seems so nervous and on edge lately," Cammie insisted. "Like last night. She nearly went to pieces over that painting. I didn't intend to upset her like that."

"I know," he replied. "It just took her by surprise. She always gets anxious when she's planning a new exhibit. I'm sure there's nothing to worry about."

His tone of voice didn't quite ring true to his words.

Cammie must have sensed this too.

"There is some connection between Sean and the portrait, isn't there?" she demanded.

The spoon he held clattered in the mixing bowl as Dad faced her determined stare. "Why do you think so?" he questioned.

Cammie's hands flew out in a gesture of exasperation. "Come on, Dad. Anyone can see the resemblance. Like two matching bookends."

"I . . . uh . . . haven't looked at that picture in several years, Cammie, not since your mother quit working on it. It may just be a coincidence."

My poor father. Somehow I knew he was skirting the issue, not wanting to lie, but unable to give a straight answer for some reason. But I was never one for subtleties.

"Who *is* the lady in the painting?" I asked point blank.

His green eyes clouded over, but then he laughed and pushed the question aside. "Hey, is this the third degree? You, Wendy, scrape these carrots, and Cammie, you tear up this lettuce."

Cammie took the head of lettuce in her hands, but she refused to give up. "Who is she?"

Dad cleared his throat and then hesitated, as though searching for words. "Just a friend of your mother's," he said finally. "From long ago, before we were married."

"What happened before we were married, Rob?" Mom asked lightly, stepping into the middle of her family. I had not heard her come into the house, and could not decide how much of the conversation she had overheard.

She walked over to Dad and lovingly brushed some flour from the tip of his nose. "On second thought, maybe you'd better not answer that question," she said with a grin.

"I plead the fifth amendment," Dad said before wrapping his arms around her slender waist. He winked at me and Cammie over his shoulder. "If I can get these girls moving, we'll have dinner shortly."

"I didn't know there was a city park in that area, Wendy," Dad said across the dinner table.

"It isn't a city park, not exactly," I explained. "It's really only a couple of vacant lots, but the people in the neighborhood use it like a playground. It's all they have. The houses there are built so close together that there isn't any place for lawns or anything. Some of the mothers take their kids there, and the bigger children play ball."

"Oh, I know the place," Dad answered. "Those houses were built right after the war when housing was so tight, and many veterans were coming home and getting married. They were just cheaply built, government subsidized, mainly intended to be temporary, I think. Then later some private contractors bought it all up for rentals. I don't suppose they do very much to take care of the neighborhood." Dad shook his head. "I even know that little piece of land you're talking about now. It's right where Fourth Street makes a curve."

"That's it, and now somebody thinks the street should be straightened out, so they're going to cut right through the park."

Mom frowned. "I don't understand your part in this," she said. "You don't have any friends in that subdivision, do you?"

My big moment had come. I caught my breath; it was now or never.

"Yes, I do . . . one . . . Mickey Decker," I finally admitted. At last, I got his name out. Rather coolly, at that, I thought.

"Mickey Decker?" Cammie was astounded. "I think

his older brother graduated with me."

I nodded, pleased that she had recognized the name. Mom was not equally impressed. Her frown remained.

"Decker? I don't remember that name, Wendy." Clearly, she was asking for more of an explanation.

I swallowed hard. "Mickey lives in Crescent Heights. That's how I know about the park. But he's so nice," I added apologetically. Now why did I do that? It wasn't necessary to defend him.

The only thing to do was to tell them the whole story and hope they would understand. I wasn't afraid of what Dad or Cammie would think, but Mom was a different story. I prayed for wisdom and courage.

I told them everything about sitting behind Mickey all year in algebra, about Project Outreach, about meeting him in the park, even about the scene in the cafeteria, about walking home with him today, and finally about the date.

Immediately, Mom shifted forward in her chair. "A date? Wendy, you accepted a date without asking me first?"

I had a tight feeling in my throat. Squirming in my seat like a naughty child, I protested weakly, "Mom, I'm not a kid anymore. I'm a sophomore in high school. You let Cammie date when she was my age. I don't see the difference."

"The difference is that we don't know this Decker boy or his family or anything about him." She looked pleadingly at Dad, but he didn't respond. "I just don't like it, Wendy. I *knew* the boys Cammie went out with. I knew their families. They were from our church. I . . ."

She paused, looked at Cammie, and then at Dad again. They were both quiet, but Cammie looked at me sympathetically.

"Are you saying that Mickey's not good enough for me to date because he's from the wrong neighborhood? Is that it?"

Mom looked at me in hurt disbelief, but she remained calm. "No, I didn't say that, Wendy. Of course, it's not that. I guess the whole idea just took me by surprise. You're so young. You've never dated before. We don't even know if he's a Christian . . ."

She was floundering, but at last Dad intervened.

"Come on, Joanna. At least, give the boy a chance. We'll meet him tomorrow when he comes for Wendy. It will be all right, I'm sure."

A single thought rushed through my mind: *Blessed are the peacemakers . . .*

"Thanks, Dad," I said, and meant it.

We finished dinner in silence. I felt as though we were going around in circles. Everything was the wrong thing to say. What was the matter with Mom?

I tried praying about it, but I didn't feel any better. Maybe God had an answer for me, and I couldn't understand it. Or maybe I had asked the wrong questions. If only there was someone to talk to. Cammie was just as much in the dark as I was. We had gotten nowhere with Dad.

Then I thought of Jane.

I needed to talk to her anyway, and, in her own strange way, she sometimes comes up with lucid and enlightening observations.

The TV in the family room was loud enough so that I could slip out the front door without being heard. No one would even know I was gone. Still there was no reason to be secretive about it, and I didn't want to risk offending my mother again. So I stuck my head in the room quickly and announced my intention.

"OK, Doodle Bug," Dad said.

No response from Mom. Maybe she was giving me the silent treatment. I deserved it after the way I had talked back to her. I would apologize later.

Jane looked like a frog.

She sat hunched in the middle of her bed with her bony knees sticking out. She held an open book in her hands and a plate of double fudge chocolate chip cookies clutched between her bare feet.

"Don't say a word!" she warned.

Chapter Seven

"Don't say a word," she repeated and sighed deeply.

Quietly I sank into the soft chintz covered chair beside her bed and watched. She sighed again.

"Well?" She jerked her head in my direction. "Aren't you going to ask me what's wrong?"

"You told me not to say anything," I defended myself.

"Oh, Wendy, how like you to nit-pick. Can't you see that I'm in agony?"

I looked at her closely. She didn't look any different than usual, but remembering my reason for coming over, I tried a sympathetic approach.

"Jane, I'm sorry. I—" My carefully planned speech was interrupted by a sudden upheaval. She bounced from the bed and started to pace the floor.

"*You're* sorry?" she demanded, flinging her arms out wide. "How do you think *I* feel? That creep!"

"What creep?"

"Russell Brown!"

"Well, how is your love life?" I asked lightly.

She had returned to the bed, pulled herself up against the headboard, and wrapped her thin arms around a pillow. Propping her chin on the cushion, she stared past me.

"It's over," she answered dramatically. "It's over, finished, done."

"You've got to be kidding. I thought the two of you . . . you seemed so right . . ." I floundered for words.

"Wendy, it's sweet of you to come over to console me, to commiserate with me, to sympathize with me, but it's no use. It's over."

I waited for the details, but, for once, she remained silent with a defeated look on her face, waiting for me to pry it out of her. So I coaxed.

"Whatever happened? Russell seemed like such a nice person," I said, biting my lip.

"Nice?" she wailed. "Oh, Wendy, he's not nice! He didn't even care about the real me at all." She rolled her eyes toward the ceiling. "Do you know what he wanted? Do you know what he really wanted?"

I shook my head.

"All he cared about was someone to copy his English homework from. Wel-l-l, he found out that I'm not that kind of girl. *No one* puts hands on my English notebook!"

Who would have believed it? My astonishment equalled my disbelief. Again I tried to be sympathetic.

"You never can tell about that kind. Those quiet ones will fool you every time," I finally managed to say. "I really am sorry, Jane."

She squared her shoulders. "It doesn't matter," she said with determination. "There are other fish in the sea. He was too short for me anyway, and even more nearsighted than I am."

"You noticed?" I giggled.

That's when she threw the pillow at me and giggled too.

"It was sweet of you to come, Wendy, but how did you know?"

"I didn't," I admitted. "Actually I came over to apologize for being angry with you for that episode in the cafeteria yesterday."

"You did look kind of silly."

It wasn't my fault rose to the tip of my tongue, but I bit my lips and remained silent. I had come to apologize.

"You're forgiven," she said gallantly. "I guess it was my fault."

"And I guess I did look kind of silly," I admitted.

"I only wish you could have seen your face when Mickey Decker came along." She laughed. "By the way, did you ever contact him about Project Outreach?"

"I thought you'd never ask," I replied smugly. Then I recounted my adventure with the soccer ball. "You were right, Jane, about God giving us the spirit of power to do whatever He asks us to do."

"Of course, I was right. I'm nearly always right. Well, what did he say?"

"He said he would come on one condition."

"Which is?"

"That I would go out with him first."

Behind her glasses, Jane's eyes grew to Frisbee size. "Knowing you, you probably said no. I don't know what I'm going to do with you, Wendy. Anyone else would be thrilled, but not you, oh, no," she rattled on. "You turned fifty shades of red and stuttered *no*."

"I said yes."

"Well, praise the Lord!" she exclaimed.

"Mom's not too happy about it though," I added.

"Not to worry," Jane assured me. "That's S.O.P. for a mother to automatically frown at the mention of a first date."

"It's not just that, Jane." I leaned forward in the chair. I didn't know whether to talk about it or not, but with Jane's amazing insight, she just might have an answer. So I told her all about Sean and the portrait and Mom's reaction.

"And it's not just that, either. Everything seems to upset her. You know she's not usually like that."

Jane agreed. "No, if there's one thing I would say about your mother, it's that she's cool, calm, and collected."

"I hope I'm exaggerating, but I'm scared. Mom's changed, and it all started when Sean came."

"Then it's elementary, Wendy," she said with one of her all-knowing looks. "I'm surprised you didn't realize it yourself."

Jane was so good at playing these cat-and-mouse games, but I knew the strategy. If I outwaited her, she would eventually make her point.

"It's really very simple."

I gave up. "If it's so simple, then why can't I figure it out for myself?" I was as dense as Jane was vague.

She smiled. "Because you have no sense for the mysterious, the romantic—"

I had heard that once too often. "I was crazy to come over here," I exploded. "I have an algebra assignment at home that makes more sense than you do."

"Wendy, calm down. And pay attention. Sean and the girl in the portrait look alike, right?"

I settled back in the chair and nodded.

"Then . . . find out who the girl in the portrait is, and you'll solve the mystery!" She sank back against the pillow and smirked.

"Good, Jane," I retorted, "but I already knew that. I asked Dad, but he wouldn't say anything. So just how do I go about finding out who she is?"

"Do I have to do everything for you, Wendy? Look through your mother's records—or catalogs—or insurance! She must have her works cataloged and insured. And then there's always her old love letters, diaries . . ." Her imagination soared out of reach.

"I can't do that," I argued. "That's snooping. I

wouldn't dare go rummaging through my mother's private papers."

She shrugged. "It's not just out of curiosity, Wendy. If you're as worried about your mother as you say, she may need help. Maybe"—her voice lowered to a dramatic whisper—"Maybe he's blackmailing her!"

I refused to believe that, but the thought of something criminal triggered a memory.

"By the way, the mystery of the bald-headed man in the yellow car is solved," I said smugly. Then I explained about Carter Crenshaw. "So, you see, he's harmless after all."

Her eyes narrowed and she chuckled. "So," she sniffed. "So, he used the old real estate agent ploy, did he?"

My well-intentioned visit to Jane had left me with a jumble of questions. Late into the night, my thoughts rode a merry-go-round.

Cammie had been horrified at Jane's suggestion. "We can't just snoop through Mom's things, Wendy," she had said. I knew she was right, but what could we do to help our mother?

I had not convinced Jane of Carter Crenshaw's innocence. But then, could he be someone other than he claimed to be?

And there was Mickey. Shyness squeezed at my heart. Could I really go on a date with him even if it was the only way to get him to participate in a Christian activity?

What and where were the answers?

My eyes blinked open and searched through the starlit darkness until I saw my Bible on the table next to me. One verse slipped into my memory: "In all thy ways, acknowledge him, and he shall direct thy paths."

"Oh, Lord, please direct my paths," I whispered as

peace at last conquered the turmoil in my brain. Before I surrendered to the heaviness of my eyelids, I remembered the one thing that Jane and I have agreed on.

"It's a good thing you told your dad about that park in Crescent Heights. If anyone knows what to do, he does."

"Petition," Dad suggested as he dished up hot oatmeal, fruit juice, and whole wheat toast. "I've been thinking about it, and I believe the best way to get started is with a petition."

He was talking about the park. "I can draft one for you and you can get everyone in the neighborhood to sign it."

"What good will that do?" I asked. I was almost late for school, but Dad always insisted that we eat breakfast.

"We'll present it to the mayor. I don't suppose there's anyone in the area with any money, is there?"

I shook my head doubtfully. "Why?"

"If we had money to hire a lawyer, we might be able to get an injunction."

I wasn't sure about the word *injunction*, but hearing Dad say *we* was very encouraging. There are few people in the world that I trust to get things done like my father.

"It would help to know how much time we have," he continued.

"I'll ask Mickey today, Dad. He's the one who talked to the surveyors."

There was a slight grimace on Mom's face when I said *Mickey*, but even that couldn't discourage me. Nor the fact that Mickey might not want to get involved in saving the park. He hadn't sounded very optimistic when we had talked about it.

My only class with him was algebra, and that was the last period of the day. Anxiously I searched the halls between classes. He had to be somewhere. Lunch with

Jane without Russell was a welcome relief, and she didn't seem to suffer too severely from a broken heart. But there was still no Mickey.

Now I really began to worry. What if he was sick? What if he didn't want to see me? And the real biggy—what if he didn't intend to date me tonight? What if that had only been his idea of a cruel joke?

The next two classes crawled by, but at last it was sixth period. With my emotions alternating between excitement and panic, I headed for room 221. My spirits plummeted at the sight of his empty desk.

After the tardy bell rang, Mickey strolled nonchalantly into class and slipped quietly into his desk. While Mr. Hardy passed out our corrected test papers, he turned around and whispered out of the corner of his mouth, "I started to cut class, but then I remembered you. We still on for tonight?"

I gulped and then nodded. Several heads turned in our direction including Mr. Hardy who had paused midway down the aisle and glared at Mickey with pursed lips. Then he pointed toward the door. This could mean only one thing—a trip to the principal's office.

"One tardy too many, Mr. Decker," he said, scowling.

Mickey stood up. "Seven o'clock," he said aloud to me and defiantly saluted our teacher before marching from the room.

Chapter Eight

I have heard stories of other girls' first dates and how their mothers hovered over them making sure they were dressed properly and offering words of advice. I was just as glad Mom didn't do this. I was already as nervous as a mosquito with hiccups, and even though my heartfelt apology had been accepted with a generous hug, she still couldn't hide her reluctance toward Mickey.

I had shampooed my hair and brushed it into a coppery sheen.

"Hold still, Wendy," Cammie cautioned as she coaxed it into soft curls with her curling iron. "You're about to come unglued. Relax."

"I can't help it," I wailed. "I'm not sure I can go through with it."

"Don't be silly, you'll be fine," she encouraged me.

Under her critical supervision, I applied a touch of blusher and mascara. She had also helped me choose my new tan slacks and yellow sweater. Her final offering was her favorite gold bracelet.

"For luck," she said, surveying me critically from head to toe before pronouncing me a success.

"You'll do," she said proudly. "Mickey should be impressed."

Exactly at seven the doorbell summoned me downstairs. Smoothing my slacks over my tummy, I glanced at myself once more in the hall mirror before reaching for the door.

I caught my breath. Leaning casually against the door frame with his arms folded across his chest, Mickey appeared as calm and self-assured as I was jittery and shy. His shoes were polished, his pants creased, and his hair was brushed away from his face. The soft, plum-colored sweater looked good enough to eat.

"Hi," he said.

"Hi," I responded, unsure how to tell him about dragging him in to meet my parents, but I didn't have to.

"I suppose the next step is to meet the folks, huh?"

I nodded. "I suppose so."

He grinned and flicked some imaginary lint from his sleeve. "Lead on."

"They're in the family room," I said. "Come on in."

I felt like I was taking the condemned man to face the firing squad as he followed me down the hall.

Dad stood up at once and offered his hand. "You must be Mickey. I'm Robert Thomsen, and this is Joanna, Wendy's mother. Sit down, please."

Mom acknowledged Mickey with a stiff nod and a forced smile. She sized him up with her eyes. If he felt as uncomfortable as I did, he did not show it.

Mickey waited until I sat down on the couch and then sat next to me. Surely Dad wasn't going to give him the third degree! I could imagine him asking such questions as what Mickey's intentions were, if he had a steady job, exactly where we were going, was he a good driver, and when did he plan to bring me home? My fears were silly.

"Wendy has told us about the playground at the end of your block. I'd like to try to help you keep it, or at least stir up a little trouble."

I hadn't had a chance to tell Mickey about Dad's interest in Crescent Heights. His face registered surprise and amusement.

Dad continued to explain about the petition.

Mickey looked questioningly at me. "A petition? For what?"

"To present to the city council," Dad answered. "We'll have to take this one step at a time. How much time do we have? Do you know when they plan to begin work?"

"I dunno. A couple of weeks maybe."

"Then the sooner the petition is circulated, the better. I expect you and Wendy should be able to handle that?"

I squirmed miserably, but Mickey shrugged and turned to me. "Can't hurt, I guess. How's Monday after school?"

Then Dad suggested, "Why not now? It won't be dark for several hours. You'll find more working people home now than you will in the afternoon. Besides, we don't have much time. If you get the petition signed tonight, I could take it to city hall on Monday. There's a city council work session Tuesday night. Perhaps the mayor would put it on the agenda."

During the entire conversation, Mom had remained rigid and silent. Suddenly she came to life.

"Robert, you can't send Wendy . . . uh, them . . . Wendy and Mickey into that neighborhood at night! What are you thinking of? It isn't safe."

I wanted to protest, but then I looked at Mickey. He silenced me with his eyes and looked directly at my mother.

Quietly he said, "Mrs. Thomsen, that happens to be my neighborhood. I live there, remember?"

Mom stammered to make some excuse. I was embarrassed for her and prayed for her to hush, but she kept on. "I know, but Wendy's different. She's not accustomed to—"

I had to stare at Mickey. Did I imagine a tightening at the corners of his mouth and a look of pain in his eyes? Or was it only my pain reflected there?

"Mrs. Thomsen, nothing's going to hurt Wendy. Believe me."

I believed him, but I don't think Mom did. She looked at Dad, but he said nothing.

"Of course," she said slowly.

Dad went into his study to get the petition. It seemed like hours before he returned with the legal-looking paper. He explained it to us and encouraged us to get as many signatures as possible.

At last Mickey and I were free to leave. In an almost inaudible whisper, Mom cautioned, "Wendy, be careful."

"It's OK," Mickey said, opening the door of the old Chevy pickup.

He had read my mind.

"I'm sorry about my mother. She—"

"Don't say anything. It's OK," he repeated. "I can live with it."

He headed the truck in the direction of Crescent Heights. Until we reached the park, the idea of actually speaking to a lot of strange people hadn't hit me. When it did, I clung to the door handle.

"I can't do it," I moaned.

Mickey quickly reached across the seat and shoved the door open. "It sticks sometimes," he said, pretending not to understand what I meant.

We spent the next two hours knocking on doors. Most of the people recognized Mickey right away, but they eyed me suspiciously. I felt the same way I had the first time in this neighborhood, as if I were a stranger and didn't really belong there.

Mickey patiently explained the petition over and over again, argued politely when necessary, and finally persuaded almost everyone to sign. He knew everybody in Crescent Heights. He had called them survivors, but they seemed very fragile to me.

We had skipped one house entirely. I didn't ask why. After we had finished all the rest, we went back to it. Mickey took my hand as we started up the short walk.

I was glad he hadn't told me sooner.

It was easy to see that Mickey had gotten his good looks from his parents. Mrs. Decker had the same high cheek bones and dark eyes. Mr. Decker was tall and slender and looked a little tired, but he welcomed me graciously into their home.

We walked straight through the front door into the living room. In places the painted wooden floor showed through a threadbare carpet. The furniture—a couch, two chairs, and a battered coffee table—was almost shabby. But although Mickey's home was very modest and different from mine, it was comfortable and spotlessly clean. There was something else too: a feeling of welcome. After the first moment of nervousness, I felt perfectly at ease.

Mickey showed the petition to his father, and they talked quietly for a moment. Mr. Decker didn't seem too eager to sign the paper. I couldn't hear what he said, but I sensed from the tone of his voice and his gestures that he needed convincing.

Somehow Mickey did this. He told me later that sometimes his father worked construction for the city, and he was afraid of losing his job.

Both Mr. and Mrs. Decker signed the petition. He was still hesitant, but she wrote her name with a defiant flourish. The two names made the total number an even thirty-five.

Mrs. Decker offered us a snack, and we sat around

the formica-topped table eating chocolate ice cream from plastic bowls. It all seemed natural and nice. Mrs. Decker asked polite questions about my family and acted surprised to learn that my mother went out to work every day, and my father stayed home and took care of the house and meals and all. She offered to share some recipes with him. I said that would be fine. Finally we left.

We had parked the truck down by the park. But when we went back to it, instead of opening the door for me to get in, Mickey led me to the old bench under the one tree that the park boasted.

"You were great with my folks," he said after he had brushed the bench off with his handkerchief and gently pulled me down beside him.

"I like them," I said. "They were so polite, not like my mother."

Mickey surprised me by planting his hand lightly against my mouth. It was not a rebuke. It was only meant to shut me up, and it did.

"Let's forget it. It's over. Let's just enjoy what's left of this evening. Not such a fun way to spend a date, was it?"

Truthfully, I had enjoyed it very much. It was pleasant to walk along with Mickey and know we were doing something worthwhile.

Mickey had one arm around my shoulder. With the fingers of his other hand, he lightly traced mine.

"I like it here at night, alone and quiet," he said softly. Then he sat up and released my hand. "You know what, Wendy? This place needs a name. Even your dad didn't know what to call it." He thought for a moment and then suggested teasingly, "What about Wendy's Place?"

I hoped he was joking about that, but he was right. *Poor little nameless park,* I thought. *Poor, little bedrag-*

gled, ugly piece of land. No wonder they want to erase you. You're just a blight, a scar. Then I had a brainstorm.

"Mickey," I cried with enthusiasm. "What this place needs more than a name is cleaning up!" I jumped from the bench and pointed in different directions. "We could pick up the litter and mow the grass and paint the bench." I could see the little plot refurbished and new and inviting. "We could plant some flowers, some more grass, put up a basketball hoop." I was breathless with excitement.

But Mickey was more realistic. "Who's going to do all this work, Wendy?"

"We are—everyone! You, me, that old couple that likes to sit here—"

"The Websters?"

I nodded. "Why not?"

"What about the money?"

"What can it cost?" I argued. "A little paint and grass seed can't be expensive." I refused to be discouraged.

Then Mickey was on his feet beside me. He took both of my hands in his and looked at me. "You're crazy, Wendy."

We stood there for a moment. Then he twirled me around and we were like two kids playing ring around the rosey. On our tiptoes, holding hands tightly, we went faster and faster until everything faded away, the scraggly grass, the litter, the splintery bench. I was so dizzy, I stumbled. Mickey steadied me in his arms.

"Crazy," he repeated, shaking his head.

When I got home a little after eleven, everything was quiet. I stopped at the door of the family room. Colors flickered on the TV screen and Dad dozed on the sofa. I turned to leave, but he must have heard me because he called, "Is that you, Wendy?"

I knew he wanted to talk about the petition, and I

promised to tell him all about it in the morning. I was savoring the joy that I had felt being with Mickey. I didn't want to spoil those feelings by talking to anyone.

Upstairs, I paused at Cammie's door. It was open, but the room was dark. I supposed that she and Sean had more exciting things to do than to sit on an old park bench and hold hands, but I wouldn't have traded my evening for anything.

Much later a noise awoke me, like a window being raised and lowered, and quick footsteps on the driveway. I didn't think about it long. I was too busy dreaming.

Chapter Nine

Strips of sunlight through the blinds tickled at my eyelids even before someone nudged me gently on the shoulder.

"Wendy, it's eight o'clock."

Through one sleepy eye, I recognized Cammie in old jeans and with a scarf hiding her hair.

I groaned, rolled over on my stomach, and hid my head under the pillow. "It's Saturday," I complained.

"We promised to clean the gallery today," she reminded me. "Mom and Dad have already left."

I had forgotten they were going to an estate sale in the country. Mom was always on the lookout for some old and unappreciated work of art to purchase.

"Dad packed a picnic lunch for them so we can eat at McDonald's or the Burger Barn," she said as she left the room.

That promise was enough to get me out of bed and into my jeans and a sweatshirt more quickly than I had thought possible.

That and the thought of asking Cammie about her date with Sean last night.

"Did you find out anything about the portrait?" I asked eagerly as we got into the station wagon.

"Not exactly," she answered with reluctance.

Patiently I waited as she backed the vehicle out of the driveway and headed in the direction of town. The suspense was too much. As she slowed down at the corner, I grilled her again.

"What do you mean by *not exactly*?"

She shook her head thoughtfully. "Sometimes I think that it's all my imagination. The truth is, Wendy, I enjoyed being with Sean so much last night that I almost forgot about the whole thing."

Cammie took advantage of a lull in the traffic to glance at me. "Can you understand that?"

I thought about Mickey and the park, and I understood completely.

But she didn't wait for an answer. "I forgot all about that silly old picture and then a certain way that Sean looked at me—" She shivered. "Well, it was just like staring into *her* eyes."

"But did you ask him about it?" I demanded.

Cammie had pulled the car into the private parking space behind the gallery.

"Well, not exactly," she said again. "I did try to get him to talk about himself, where he came from, and things like that. But he just brushed it aside and started talking about me or—" She hesitated as she drew the key from the ignition and dumped it in her purse.

"Or what?"

"He asked a lot of questions about Mom. And you know what's odd, Wendy?" She turned and looked quizzically at me. "I don't know any answers. She's never talked about herself. She doesn't have any family, at least not that I know of. We really don't know much about her, do we? I mean, she's our own mother."

I had never really thought about it before, but Cammie was right.

Cammie unlocked the back door of the building to

let us in. To our left was the small workroom with empty frames and canvases. Mom's office was off to the right. Down a short narrow hall was the main room where the walls were filled from the floor to ceiling with pictures carefully arranged in groups according to style, subject, or artist. The rich mauve-colored carpet and the muted gray walls denoted a quiet elegance. Everywhere I sensed my mother's touch, and concern tugged at my heart.

"I'm glad Dad took Mom out this morning. Maybe getting away from everything will bring her back down to earth," I theorized.

"Maybe," Cammie agreed, heading for the utility closet. "Do you want to vacuum or dust?"

"Neither," I replied honestly. "I want to find out who the girl in the painting is."

"Well, so do I," Cammie said, pulling the vaccum out into the hall. "But that's not why we're here."

"Cammie, aren't you curious?"

She had stooped down to plug the cord into an outlet. When she raised up, something besides curiosity was mirrored in her dark eyes.

"To be truthful, Wendy, it's worse than that. I'm worried. But I don't know what to do about it. We asked Dad, and he wouldn't give us a straight answer."

I took a deep breath and felt a flush creep up my face before I suggested, "We could look through Mom's papers or records or something."

"Wendy!" Cammie cried in dismay. "I've already told you no."

I shrugged. "I know, I know. It's a dumb idea and not right, but Jane—"

Cammie frowned. "I don't know why you brought Jane in on this. What exactly did you tell her, and, for heaven's sake, Wendy, why?" she demanded with more than a hint of exasperation.

"I told her I was worried about Mom. I told her—" I stared at my shoes. "I guess I told her everything, about Sean and the portrait and how upset Mom got," I confessed sheepishly. "I don't know why exactly. It's just hard to keep things from Jane."

I stood there repentant, digesting the look of extreme chagrin on Cammie's face.

"Did you ever stop to think that it's none of Jane's business? Or even yours or mine?" She thrust a feather duster in my face. "And we certainly will not go poking about in Mom's private papers."

I received both the utensil and her reprimand in shameful silence.

Then her attitude softened and a forgiving smile lit her face. "I'm sorry for jumping at you, Wendy. I know you're worried too. Something is strange, and Mom's not herself. But I keep thinking it surely can't be anything that terrible. If it were, why would Mom be sponsoring an art exhibit for Sean?"

I chewed my lip and tried to sound casual as I mumbled, "Jane said it might be blackmail."

Cammie's smile died. "Blackmail?" she snapped. "Do you honestly think that Mother has something to hide?"

"You said yourself that we didn't know much about her," I defended myself.

"Dust!" she commanded and flung her arm in the direction of the main gallery. The vacuum roared as she pushed it hard down the length of the hall. Smarting from her stern dismissal, I set about my own task. We worked quietly for an hour until Cammie was satisfied with the results.

As I waited for her to replace the vacuum in the closet, the phone rang.

"Get that, will you, Wendy?" she called from the utility room. "Take a message if you need to."

Quickly I stepped into the office and picked up the receiver.

"Thomsen Gallery."

"Hello, is this Mrs. Joanna Thomsen?"

It was a man's voice, a man's voice that I had heard before.

"No, it isn't," I said. "The gallery is closed and Mrs. Thomsen is out of town for the day."

"I see." He paused. "Perhaps, you could tell me when she will return?"

"She won't be back in the shop until Monday, but I'll be happy to tell her you called." As I talked, I rummaged through the top desk drawer for a pencil. In my haste, I pulled the entire thing from the desk and emptied the contents on the floor. At last armed with pencil and pad, I returned to the phone conversation.

"If you'll tell me who you are and what you need, I'll be glad to give her the message," I said, with the pencil poised over the paper.

But the only answer was a click as the connection was ended.

Cammie stuck her head through the office door. "Who was it, Wendy?"

"I'm not sure," I answered slowly. "But I think it was that real estate agent. "What's his name . . . Mr. . . ?"

"Crenshaw?" Cammie supplied. "I thought Mom would have gotten rid of him by now. Did he leave a message?"

"No, no message," I answered and fell to my knees to straighten up the jumbled mess on the floor.

"Here, I'll help," Cammie volunteered and knelt beside me.

We sorted the paper, pens, pencils, paper clips, and replaced them in the empty drawer. To one side was a small wadded up piece of white fabric.

"I wonder what this is," Cammie murmured, taking

it in her hand and carefully unfolding the corners. Finally the cloth lay open in her hand, revealing a small gold heart.

"How strange," she whispered, touching the piece of jewelry with the tip of her finger. "There's something engraved here."

With one end of the fabric, she polished the piece of gold and scrutinized it again. Then, extending her hand, she allowed me to see for myself. In elaborate script, so delicate and worn that it was barely readable, was the inscription: *To Joanna with love from Crystal.*

I almost stopped breathing and watched as Cammie turned it over in her palm. "It's a locket," she declared, "or at least half of a locket."

"Crystal?" I questioned as we stared at the small black and white snapshot. Even void of color, it was unmistakably the girl in the portrait.

Cammie nodded. Then she raised her head. Her eyes met mine. "Wendy, isn't the girl in the painting wearing a locket?"

I tried to remember, but only her haunting eyes came vividly to my mind. I shook my head. "I don't know," I admitted.

"I'm sure she is. But there's one way to find out." Quickly she refolded the cloth and crammed the locket back into the back corner of the drawer. Then she slammed it shut.

"Come on. We're going home."

Once in the station wagon, we sped through the narrow alley behind the gallery. The tires squealed as we screeched to a stop before entering the street.

"Cammie!" I shrieked. "What's the hurry? The portrait isn't going anywhere."

She blinked at me and then breathed deeply. "You're right, Wendy. I don't know what got into me."

From then on, she drove carefully until we reached Avondale Drive. Leaving the automobile in the garage, we went in through the kitchen. There was no need for directions as I followed Cammie's rapid steps down the hallway toward the studio and straight for the small storage room.

She threw open the door and came to a jolting standstill. I was so close behind her that it almost threw me off balance. She glanced swiftly around the room, then walked over to the partially open window. I watched as she swiped her finger through a smudge of dirt on the sill and clenched her hand in a tight fist. Finally she turned to me. Her face was drained of color and her eyes were wide in the same questioning disbelief that gripped me tightly.

The easel was empty!

Chapter Ten

Silently we left the studio and wandered back into the kitchen. Cammie dropped into a chair at the table, her face in her hands. Then she raised her head, took a deep breath, and admitted reluctantly, "Wendy, *I* left the window open."

I stared at her wide-eyed as she explained. "It was so hot and stuffy in there the other day when I took Sean into the studio. He said the heat wasn't good for the oil paint." Then she sighed guiltily. "I meant to go back later and close it, but I forgot."

"And someone just happened to climb through the window and take the painting?" I cried.

"I know it doesn't make sense, Wendy," Cammie reasoned, "for anyone to steal a painting of an unknown girl—" She stopped in midsentence, remembering. Intuition gleamed in her eyes. "Except, of course, we know now that it isn't just some unknown girl. The thief knew exactly what he was doing."

"Sean?" I whispered.

Cammie shuddered. "How could it be anyone else? If only we knew why."

"Should we tell Mom?" I asked.

She contemplated that for a moment. "No, not now."

I protested, "But don't you think she has a right to know?"

"Of course, she does, but not yet." Her eyes clouded with anxiety. "Can't you just imagine what this would do to her?"

Nervously she pulled the scarf from around her head and shook her dark hair loose. Then she stood up, twisting the scarf in her hands. "I've got to find some way to get the painting back first."

"But you don't know where it is?" I exclaimed, the tone of my voice ending in a question mark.

"I think I do," she replied quietly and left the kitchen.

I knew she didn't intend for me to follow, so I stayed behind to look for something to eat. The feeling of panic that had gripped my insides had subsided into pangs of hunger. Visions of Big Macs teased me, but there was no chance for that now, so I settled for peanut butter.

I was sitting at the table with the opened jar and a spoon when Cammie returned, dressed in light blue slacks and a soft white blouse.

"I called Sean," she announced. "He's on his way over."

The spoon clinked on the bottom of the jar as I stared at her doubtfully. "He's coming here?" I asked.

Before she could answer, the chimes rang. I waited until I heard their footsteps in the hall before I followed them uninvited, toward the studio.

Cammie led Sean to the storage room and jerked open the door with more drama than necessary. He stood there with his arms folded casually. The only emotion visible in his face was uncertainty. He surveyed the small area with his eyes before gazing at Cammie and holding out his hands in a questioning gesture.

"The portrait's gone," she said.

He shrugged. "I see that. Your mother was smart to

move it. This is a very poor place to keep a valuable painting."

Cammie blinked rapidly and then turned to meet my puzzled glance. Had we both jumped to the wrong conclusion? A smile of relief relaxed the frown lines on Cammie's forehead, but I refused to believe him.

"It's been stolen," I insisted.

Sean dropped his hands and whirled around to face me. His mouth formed the word *who* even before it was audible.

I stammered, "Maybe *you* know who's taken it."

I was startled by my own daring, and Cammie's face registered annoyance.

"Then you don't *know* that it was stolen?" Sean asked evenly, regaining his composure. "Or when?"

Cammie shook her head, but something clicked in my brain. I knew when. Last night. The noise I had heard when I was half asleep repeated itself in my brain. But I kept the information to myself. It would be pointless to make any accusations without proof.

"I'm sure you're right," Cammie said. "Mom must have moved it."

She may have believed him, but I was unconvinced. I tried once again.

"Was the girl in the painting wearing a small gold locket?"

Sean considered my question carefully before he replied, "I don't know. I only saw the portrait once."

I sensed some evasiveness in his answer, but I let it go unchallenged and left the studio. Later I heard them leave the house together.

Confronting Sean had accomplished nothing. His solution was too easy. I wandered aimlessly through the house trying to piece the puzzle together. At least we had a name for the girl in the picture—Crystal. Dad had said she was a friend of Mom's. *With love* the inscription had read. A dear friend, I concluded. But what was her relationship to Sean? If Mom knew (as she surely did), why did she refuse to acknowledge it? Why did Sean deny taking the painting? And where was the other half of the locket? The why's, who's, where's, and what's spun around in my head like the lead paragraph of a news article.

The silence of the house was depressing. I had one last book report due before the end of school. Perhaps reading would distract me for a while. It was too nice a day to be inside anyway. I took my book and my cassette player out to the gazebo. This little summer house of lattice framework construction set back from our home in a circle of trees was one of my favorite places to get away to think.

For the first day of May, it was unusually warm and muggy with a hint of rain in the air, but the tree-shaded gazebo was comfortable and cool and quiet. I sank into one of the cushioned seats and opened *A Tale of Two Cities*. "It was the best of times; it was the worst of times . . ." seemed an appropriate way to describe my own life.

The good part was Mickey. In the excitement of the morning I had forgotten all about him and the park. My very first date had been nothing like I had ever imagined, but I shivered a little thinking about it. I had kept my part of the bargain. Now he would have to come to the Project Outreach party and mingle with my Christian friends. I prayed earnestly that they would become his friends as well. I knew that above all else, Mickey needed Jesus. Oh, if only I could be the one to help him realize that!

I whispered his name to God and thanked God for the spirit of power that gave me the courage to talk to Mickey.

The bad part was still my mother. Nothing had been settled. I prayed for her and for Cammie too. A feeling of peace replaced the heartfelt tremors of the morning. It would be all right. Mom would be all right. I knew.

Turning the pages of the book, I lost myself in the French Revolution until I heard my parents' car in the driveway.

I explained to them that Cammie had gone for a drive with Sean. Mom frowned but said nothing. Dad headed for the kitchen.

"Come with me, Wendy," he invited. "You promised to tell me how things went last night."

Proudly I brought him the petition with thirty-five names on it, and I tried to tell him about the people in Crescent Heights.

He nodded his head with understanding. "Well, this is a start, Wendy. I'll deliver it to the mayor on Monday morning. Then we'll just have to wait. And pray," he added, opening the refrigerator.

Cammie came to the kitchen in time for dinner. Mom seemed more relaxed after spending a day with Dad, and I silently thanked God for that.

But the serenity of the meal was abruptly broken when Mom questioned Cammie about spending so much time with Sean. "Your audition will be here before you know it. You need your time for your music," she reminded her.

Misreading her concern, Cammie answered Mom more harshly than she deserved. "I have *time* enough to clean the gallery," she retorted. Then she jumped up from the table, threw her napkin down, and fled to the music room. I knew it was not just for practice. Playing the piano has always been an outlet for her emotions.

Mom said nothing more except to offer to help Dad with the dishes. I retreated to my room.

Too keyed up to read, I absently skimmed through

the pages of my book. I had just reached the part when Sydney Carton changes places with Charles Darnay in the Bastille when Cammie came into my room and closed the door. Her visit did not surprise me. I knew we had to talk.

"No munchies tonight, Wendy?" she began in a light-hearted way, flopping down in the bentwood rocker by my bed.

I glanced at her over the pages of the book and shook my head. "Not hungry," I mumbled.

"Me either," she replied, drumming her fingertips nervously on the arm of the chair. "Only more confused."

"Did you really buy Sean's idea that Mom removed the painting?" I asked doubtfully.

She nodded, "I want to. It makes more sense than anything else."

"Why?" I asked.

"Why! I'm so tired of that word," she exploded. "I'm tired of the whole charade. Being with Sean this afternoon almost made me forget, and worse, it almost made me not care anymore." Her bottom lip quivered.

She sighed loudly. "Well, Wendy, what am I going to do?"

"About what?"

"My life," she answered. "I didn't mean to dump on Mom like that. I don't want to hurt her ever, but I'm just not sure about the conservatory anymore." Her onyx eyes filled with tears. Huddled in the big chair in a long pink granny gown, she seemed suddenly small and defenseless.

"Is it because of Sean?"

She sighed again. "Maybe, I've enjoyed being with him and doing something else besides working at that piano every day. But I had thought about this even before he came along. I want to go to college," she announced.

"I had intended to tell Mom, but now I don't know how."

She stood up and walked over to the window, staring into the cloudy night. "No stars," she muttered.

Then she paced anxiously around the room. "I love my music," she said, more to herself than to me, "but I don't know if I can make that my whole life. I need more time to think. I'm only nineteen." Then she twirled around and exclaimed, "You're so lucky, Wendy! I've always envied you."

"Me?" I asked with disbelief. "*You* envy *me*? Why?"

She flung her hands out and open. "You've always been free to do whatever you wanted. No one ever forced you into a niche and made you stay there forever."

My mouth dropped open in astonishment. "But, Cammie, that's only because I'm no good at anything. All I ever wanted was to be like the rest of you," I protested.

A smile brightened her tear-streaked face. "You silly goose. You're worth more than the rest of us put together. You'll see someday. All you need is a little self-confidence."

Tossing my book aside, I scooted over to the edge of the bed to be closer to her. My heart skipped with excitement. "Do you really think so?"

"I wouldn't say it if I didn't. It's like this park." She searched my face for a spark of understanding. "I mean, how many other people would spend time caring about a hopeless piece of dirt?"

She propped a pillow against the headboard and settled herself more comfortably on my bed before she went on talking in a philosophical tone.

"All the artists in the world are no good without the people like you who keep things going. If I can't play the piano, I'm certainly not going to turn the pages for someone else," she admitted honestly. "But you're different, Wendy. Nothing would get done without the quiet caring ones like you who avoid the spotlight but who can see beyond a sheet of music or a piece of canvas and recognize the practical things that have to be done. I wish I were more like you," she added sincerely.

I sank back against my pillow beaming with gratitude. "Thanks, Cammie," I said. "That really makes me feel better."

She laughed. "What are big sisters for?"

Drawing her legs up close to her body, she clasped her hands around them and rested her chin on her knees. For a moment she stared pensively into space.

"OK, that takes care of you; now what are we going to do to make *me* feel better?" she asked lightly. Then the bright quality of her voice faded as she answered her own question.

"Don't tell me," she warned. "I know the first step is to tell Mom. It's just so hard." Once again tears moistened her eyes. "I've tried praying about it, but it hasn't helped much. I used to think Mom was just about perfect. Lately she's so different, ever since—"

The sentence trailed off unfinished, but I knew what she meant.

"Since Sean came?" It was an endless circle.

Lifting her head, she turned to me. "Why do you think she resents him so?"

"But she brought him here, and she arranged the show for him," I reminded her.

"I know." Cammie looked puzzled. "That's what makes it all so crazy. It's almost as if she owes him something. It always comes back to the same thing."

"Mom, Sean, and . . ." I hesitated. "I still think he took the painting."

She didn't argue with me this time. I looked at her thoughtfully.

"Dad knows something," I concluded.

Cammie agreed. "But he won't betray Mom. Sean

denies everything." Her mouth quivered. "We can't ask Mom."

"It seems like a dead-end, doesn't it?"

As Cammie nodded, a light patter of rain splashed the window.

"I hate this weather," she said, shivering.

Instinctively I reached down to the foot of the bed and pulled up the thick comforter, drawing it close around both of us.

In its warmth, Cammie settled back against the pillow. "Do you remember, Wendy, when we were little girls and shared the same room? When we were scared or the weather was bad, you always climbed into bed with me."

I grinned at the pleasant memory, but it seemed forever ago.

"It was nice then, before life became so complicated," I answered.

Cammie's eyes were closed. The dark lashes rested like half-moons on her face, "I wish we could go back," she murmured sleepily. "I wish we could be children again."

I picked up my book and opened it. I wished I could trade places with Cammie like Sydney and Charles did. But things like that happen only in books.

Cammie spoke once more. "I don't believe he's a thief. He's too kind and gentle . . ."

Chapter Eleven

"According to the mayor, the city planner, and their maps, there is no such thing as a park in the Crescent Heights subdivision," Dad announced as he dropped cauliflower and broccoli into a steamer.

I couldn't hide my look of disappointment. Mickey had collected some more signatures the day before, and Dad had taken the petition with forty-three names on it to Mayor Dennison.

"But what about the people who've turned it into a park?" I asked. "What is that property, anyway?"

Dad shrugged. "Just vacant lots that have been confiscated for payment of back taxes."

"What can we do now, Dad? Did the mayor care at all?"

Dad tried to cheer me up. "The truth is that he was sympathetic. He promised to present it at the next work meeting." He reached out and patted my arm. "We won't give up yet. We just have to prove that there's a need for a park there."

I sighed in frustration. "They would know that if they ever went by and saw all those people there."

"You're right," Dad responded. "I drove by the 'park'

myself today, but you must admit it's nothing much to look at."

"That's exactly what I told Mickey. We've got to clean it up and improve it so that it looks like something better than two abandoned lots."

Dad vigorously chopped more raw vegetables before looking at me again. "I agree with you, Wendy, and I don't want to dampen your enthusiasm, but have you considered the cost?"

It was the same question Mickey had asked. I had the same answer. "Grass seed can't be that expensive."

Dad nodded. "I wasn't thinking about seed. I was thinking of you. Are you willing to take a chance on getting hurt?"

The cautious tone of his voice worried me. "You're over my head. What do you mean?"

He hesitated, choosing his words carefully. "Do you realize that others might not want to get involved? That they might not care as much as you do? And do you understand the real reason why you're doing this? Is it to prove something to yourself or Mickey or is it really to help the people of Crescent Heights?"

I couldn't explain to him the feelings that I had had when I first discovered Crescent Heights that day of the track tryouts, that immediate identification with something as down-and-out as I was. "I'm not sure I know why," I admitted. "But I'm sure that it's right."

Dad was silent for a minute, then he said quietly, "I'm proud of you, Doodle Bug. Do you know that caring for others is the essence of Christianity? Reaching out to them unselfishly is one of the requirements of discipleship."

An image of bearded men in long robes and sandals flashed through my mind. "Disciples?"

Dad nodded. "We are all called to be that," he said.

Suddenly I felt small and inadequate. "I never

thought about it like that. But *I* can't be a disciple," I stammered.

"Don't underestimate yourself. Even Simon Peter wasn't always a rock." He smiled. "Now I've got to get dinner ready."

"I'm sorry if this is taking too much time away from your book, Dad," I apologized.

He reassured me with a quick hug. "Nonsense. It's just what I needed. I had reached a plateau, no new ideas and tired of the old ones. Everyone needs a diversion occasionally."

It was then that I realized the Cammie was not practicing. I looked at my father questioningly.

"Even your sister," he answered with a mysterious twinkle in his eyes.

Worrying about the park was my diversion, I supposed. At the moment it seemed to have more substance than the missing painting, the locket, and the episode with Sean.

Cammie came in a little later and went immediately to the music room. She was practicing intently when I heard Mom's car in the driveway. I didn't know if she wanted to keep Mom from knowing she hadn't been working on her music, or if she was afraid Mom would discover she had been out with Sean. Maybe it was one and the same thing. I didn't question her motives. I only felt sorry for her, torn between her loyalty to Mom and her friendship to Sean. Thank goodness, I didn't have to choose between practicing the piano and seeing Mickey. There would be no contest. Sometimes being non-talented had its advantages.

Mickey answered my phone call after dinner with a question. "Good news or bad?"

"Both, Mickey. The mayor was sympathetic, to quote

Dad, but the park isn't really a park, at least not according to 'his honor.' "

"So, it's City Hall—1 and Crescent Heights—0. I knew it was a waste of time." He was more than disappointed; he was bitter.

I wanted to reassure him. "Wait a minute. That wasn't the end of the ball game. Mayor Dennison did promise to bring it up at the meeting tomorrow night."

Mickey agreed to come over and make some plans for cleaning up the park, but not without some hesitation.

"What about your mother?" he asked.

"I thought you said you could live with it. She won't throw sticks and stones at you. Don't be a coward," I teased.

After dinner Mom and Dad went for a walk, so Mickey and I had the family room to ourselves. Wanting to appear super organized, I had laid out a pad and pencil to write down everything we decided.

The first heading was *Litter*.

"That's easy," Mickey said. "My little sisters and some of their friends can take care of it. I'll promise them a Coke or something."

"That smacks of bribery," I said, laughing. "But it's OK with me. I know some of the kids from church will help too if I ask them."

Mickey frowned. "Project Outreach?" he asked, but he didn't argue.

"A couple of garbage bags should handle that." Beside the heading *Litter*, I wrote *Mickey's sisters and PO committee* and *garbage bags*.

At the end of an hour, we had what I considered a well-organized plan. At least it looked good on paper.

1. Litter	Mickey's sisters PO Committee	garbage bags

2. Old grass	Mickey	Dad's mower
3. New grass	Dad??	grass seed
4. Flowers	Mrs. Decker	transplant from her yard??
5. Bench	Mr. Webster??	spray paint

I was pleased to see it all there in black and white. We planned to begin the next day.

When my parents came in, Dad stopped in the family room to see us. He approved of our plans. He also agreed to furnish the grass seed and to plant it.

"It won't sprout quickly enough for the mayor or commissioners to see it, but we can stake it out and tie strings around the area, so at least they will be aware of our intentions. I'll have to convince one of them to come look at it, but I used to play golf with John Anderson. I'll give him a call tomorrow."

"Dr. Thomsen," Mickey began, "do we really have a chance?"

"I think so," Dad replied encouragingly. "But there is one resource we have overlooked."

"What's that?" I thought we had covered everything.

"The media," he answered. "TV, newspapers. If we could get some interest generated with them, then the public would get involved. It's a good human interest story."

For some reason, Mickey didn't look too enthusiastic, but it seemed like a perfect solution to me. In fact, it sounded so good that I offered to be the one to bring it to the attention of the press. Dad was pleased.

"But the sooner, the better," he cautioned. "It might be well if the newspapers or TV could get shots of you at work."

The look in Mickey's eyes disturbed me. Even though he hadn't voiced an objection, I could sense his reluctance.

"I'll do it tomorrow. Now I can add something to the list for me."

So I triumphantly wrote:

6. News media Wendy telephone

Dad smiled approvingly. "I haven't had this much fun since my first book was published."

I was ecstatic, Dad was pleased, but Mickey was quiet. He halfheartedly agreed to walk over to the Burger Barn for a soft drink. We trudged along in an uncomfortable silence. I waited for him to reach out and take my hand, but he didn't.

We were at the end of the driveway before he placed his arm around my shoulders. "Do you really want to go to the Burger Barn, Wendy? I really need to talk things over alone with you."

I knew the perfect place. "Come on," I invited. "I know a good place to talk."

I took his hand and pulled him along to our backyard. The perfect place was the gazebo. The sun was setting, and shadows caused by the twilight coming through the lattice strips made light and dark crisscrosses on his face. I tried to read the expression in his eyes. I could not imagine the reason for the anger mirrored there, nor the hurt. But I knew they were real.

Minutes dragged by before he spoke. "Your dad thinks this is fun?"

I remembered that Dad had said something about it being fun. He hadn't meant to offend Mickey, but I realized that he had taken it differently.

He stood up and walked across the wooden floor away from me. He raised both arms and gripped the entrance of the gazebo with each hand. The muscles tensed across his shoulders. Then he relaxed and turned back to me.

"Why do we have to call in the newspapers and TV? Is he trying to turn this into some kind of three-ring circus, with me and my neighborhood as the main attraction?"

I could feel but not comprehend the bitter reproach in his voice. I defended my father. "He was only trying to help."

"Sure, he was. Let the whole world see the poor people of Crescent Heights."

Now I was angry. "You've got it all wrong," I insisted.

"No, Wendy, *you've* got it all wrong. Your dad is just as bad as your mother, only he's more sneaky about it."

"Oh, Mickey, you're wrong," I repeated, at a loss for words. "He . . . we . . ." I searched for the right thing to say. "Do you know Jesus?"

He looked startled. "Why?" he asked with hostility. "What does that have to do with anything?"

"It has everything to do with it. I only realized that today." I tried to explain to him what Dad had said to me about loving and caring for others. "So you see," I concluded, "you're mistaken about Dad. He cares. I'm not so sure about you anymore."

The accusation stung. His mood changed abruptly and he walked toward me. He cupped my face in his hand.

"Wendy, I do care, more than you can know. But we have some pride too. Signing petitions, going to the mayor, that's one thing. It has some dignity to it, but calling in a TV camera, I don't know. It just hit me wrong. Like we were going on display or something. Then when your dad made that crack about it being fun—well, it's not a question of fun with me. You don't know what it's like to be the poor kid, to have to constantly prove yourself. How could you know, living in that house? That Christian stuff's all right for you, but what does God care about me?"

"So much, Mickey," I whispered. "He cares so much."

"OK," he said, sitting down beside me and taking my hand in his. "You're probably right, your dad's right.

Call in the TV and the newspapers and whatever else it takes. The park is important to the kids. Swallowing my pride isn't easy, but I can try."

I wanted to believe him, but I didn't, not really. He didn't say another word. He left me alone in the gazebo.

What I had thought was a perfect evening had been spoiled by misunderstanding and misguided pride. Maybe this was what Dad had warned me about. In his own way, Mickey was prejudiced, too; only he couldn't quite see it.

My dreams that night were of circuses. I could see Mickey being led around a ring with a chain on his neck and little dark-haired children with ruffled collars performing like trained animals. My father was the ring master cracking a whip and inviting the audience to view the spectacle.

I awoke before dawn with the covers in a jumble. Somehow I felt like a failure again. Why was it that I never succeeded at anything that I set out to do? Mickey didn't know it, wouldn't have understood even if I had tried to explain it to him. But I knew what it felt like to be different. I had felt that way most of my life.

Through the window I watched the sun signal the creation of a new day.

In all thy ways acknowledge Him . . .

Pulling the blanket tightly around me, I closed my eyes and prayed for Mickey and then for myself.

Chapter Twelve

I dreaded seeing Mickey at school that day. All through lunch I let Jane do the talking. Her despair over Russell Brown had been eclipsed by the excitement of having her braces removed that afternoon. I tried to share her enthusiasm, but I had such butterflies that even the best junk food the cafeteria had to offer failed to cheer me up.

My fears were groundless. Mickey smiled at me as he sat down in his desk sixth period and turned sideways to talk to me as though nothing had happened.

"Are you all set for work today? My sisters and some of their friends will be waiting for us right after school. Uh . . ." he added hesitantly, "did you call the TV station?"

I shook my head as the tardy bell rang. An explanation would have to wait.

"We'll only do it if we have to," I told him later. "If it's necessary, we'll contact them. If not, we won't." It had taken half a night of restless tossing and turning to arrive at this simple solution.

Mickey seemed relieved. "What'd your dad say?"

"He said I could do whatever I wanted to. It doesn't matter. This is our project, not his."

I felt guilty cutting my father down like that, but I couldn't risk hurting Mickey's feelings again. Besides, Dad had understood better than I when I had told him.

The weather was perfect for working outside, not cold and not too warm. On the cement-block porch of their house, crowded close together, Mickey's three sisters and four of their friends sat patiently waiting for us after school.

It was the first time I had met the Decker girls. Mickey introduced them to me individually and with some ceremony. Anna was the oldest, then Sherry, and finally Cindy, who was only five. They were younger, prettier versions of their mother with dark, shiny hair, sparkling eyes, and shy smiles.

As we reached the walk to their home, Mrs. Decker came to the door and asked if we would like to come in for something to drink.

"We'll need it worse later, Mama," Mickey said. "I don't think we'd better put this work force off any longer."

Ron Peters and Troy Davis, two of my friends from church, were already at the park. They separated the children into two groups and gave each a garbage bag. The path through the park was a natural dividing line. Ron and Mickey supervised one side, and Troy and I took the other. As they worked, Ron talked to Mickey. I couldn't hear what he was saying, but I knew he never missed an opportunity to witness. I didn't have to hear Mickey's response. I could see him scowl and shake his head.

"Oh, Mickey," I whispered, "please listen."

Quickly the bottles and paper disappeared. Picking up the trash was a game for the eager little girls. In almost no time, the place was spotless.

Luckily, Mr. and Mrs. Webster were in their usual place on the old bench. Mickey and I took time to talk to them and tell them what we were doing. Mr. Webster's face crinkled in a smile at the idea of repainting the bench.

"I don't know why I didn't think of that myself. It seems like Mother here"—he indicated his wife with a grin—"and I use it the most. A fresh coat of paint would make it sit better."

He turned to his wife and spoke to her in a loud voice. "Don't you think so, Mother?" Then he laughed at his own joke as she smiled and nodded.

"Hard of hearing," he explained. "I'll even go you one better, Mickey. There's an old picnic table in our backyard, just about the same shape as the bench. If you think we could get it moved out here, I'll just fix it up with a little paint too and donate it to the cause."

"That's great, Mr. Webster," I broke in. "We could put it right here under the tree."

Everything was falling into place. Hopefully, the mayor and city commissioners would be impressed.

Calling all the children together, Mickey congratulated them on their fine work. "And in celebration, we're all going over to the Burger Barn for a treat. I'll go back and get the truck." Then he turned to me. "And on the way back, we'll stop off at your house and get the mower. There's still time left to get the grass cut today."

"That's not necessary," Troy said. "I brought a mower." He motioned toward his own pickup. "I'll get this little bit of grass cut in no time."

Mickey watched Ron and Troy suspiciously as they headed toward their truck.

"Why?" he demanded. "Why're they doing this?"

Disciples, I thought, but Mickey wouldn't understand that. "Because I asked them to," I answered simply. "Maybe because they care too."

Mickey shook his head in disbelief as he trudged down the street to his house.

The five older kids promised to sit still in the back of the truck. The two youngest squeezed in up front with us. Cindy nestled in my lap. I held her small body close to me and wrapped my arms around her. Her hair smelled fresh and clean. I looked across the seat at Mickey and smiled.

"I liked your friends, Wendy," he admitted hesitantly.

I grinned. "And I like your sisters." I gave Cindy another hug and she giggled.

Ordering soft drinks and four different flavors of ice cream was a little hectic, but eventually we all settled down to enjoy the special treats. I tried to share the cost with Mickey.

"No way," he declared. "This is my expense, even if it wasn't on the list."

"Speaking of lists," I said, reaching into my purse and taking out the one we had made. "Watch this." Triumphantly I crossed off the first entry.

When we stopped at my house, Mickey said, "I'll call you later. Maybe we can do some algebra or something. Maybe I can make up to you for last night."

Reluctantly I told the little girls goodbye. Cindy put her arm around my neck and planted a sticky kiss. "Bye, Wendy," she said. "Will you come see me again?"

I promised her that I would.

Dad was pleased with the report of our afternoon's work.

"Good, Wendy. And I'll have to tell you what I've done." He sounded mysterious, looking like the cat who had swallowed the canary, but I had to wait until he set the timer on the oven before he revealed his secret.

"This morning I went to the park and took some pictures," he announced.

"Pictures?" I asked incredulously. "What for?"

"Before and after," he exclaimed. "We should have thought of it before. What will it prove to show the park after it's cleaned up if no one knows how bad it looked before?" He beamed proudly.

I had always known my father was smart, but now he took on genius status. I could even forgive him for all the healthy food he had fed me for the last few years.

I left the kitchen and went into my room to get cleaned up. Once again there was a noticeable silence from the music room. Just then the phone rang. Thinking it must be Mickey, I made a mad dash for it.

"Oh, Wendy, good, I'm glad it's you," Cammie said. "Is Mom home yet?"

"No," I answered. "Why?"

"I'm not coming home right away, and I thought maybe you could tell her that Sean is taking me out to dinner. I'll be home later. It's no big deal. Just tell her."

She hung up before I had a chance to protest.

I met Mom at the bottom of the stairs. She took the news in silence. But she was not silent when I told her that Mickey was coming over later.

"It seems like both of you have reached that point when you don't ask permission anymore!" she snapped. "You just *tell* me what you are doing."

I could tell she was hurt. An apology was definitely in order. Cammie may have been old enough to run her own life, but I was only fifteen.

"I know I should have cleared it with you first. We've got finals coming up next week. He's only coming over to study."

It wasn't a very persuasive argument, even if it was true.

"Wendy, it's not smart to spend all your time with one boy when you're so young. I don't like the idea of dating on a school night, but I suppose studying is all right. There's not much I can do about it now."

"I'm sorry, Mom," I said, trying to keep the tears from spilling down my face. "I really should have asked."

Then, her irritation spent, she put both hands on my shoulders and stared into my face. "I'm sorry too, my dear Wendy. I'm really not trying to be mean." She sighed deeply. "It just seems that everything's changing. Forgive me?" she asked.

As I nodded, too overcome to speak, she drew me to her and held me tightly in a motherly caress. With my face nestled against the smooth silk of her blouse, I heard her whisper, "I can't hold on to you forever. You're growing up so—"

The ring of the telephone stopped her. Dad hurried in from the kitchen. "It's for you, Joanna."

"Is it Cammie again?"

"No," he answered her quietly. "It's Carter Crenshaw."

I could feel her tremble. "I can't talk to him, Rob," she said adamantly as she released me.

"Perhaps you'd better, Jo," he coaxed.

She shook her head, and, grasping the bannister for support, started up the stairs. "Tell him . . . tell him anything. I won't speak to him."

With a tight feeling in my throat, I watched her make her way up the steps, then turned back to Dad. But he had disappeared.

"Well, I guess you're so busy with your new-found love, you don't have time for old friends anymore," Jane greeted me contemptuously the next morning, but her teeth were bared in an outrageous smile.

Then I remembered that I had promised to come over the night before. But Mom's reaction to that phone call had completely erased it from my mind. Besides, Mickey had come over. It would not be difficult to choose between seeing him and inspecting Jane's mouth even if it did represent an orthodontic miracle.

"Jane, I'm sorry," I apologized. "You look great. I

would hardly have recognized you."

"Probably because you haven't seen me for so long!" she reprimanded me. "However, I agree with you." Now she broke into a real smile. "I can't tell you what a relief it is to get all that metal out of my mouth. Even food tastes different."

We were in the lunch room as usual. I *had* been neglecting Jane recently. To make up for it, I told her all about the park and what we had done and planned to do.

"That doesn't sound like my idea of an exciting social life," she commented. "But to each her own, I guess. How did you ever get Mickey Decker involved in that?"

Her question surprised me. "Why?"

She shrugged. "He just doesn't seem like the type."

I grinned. "Jane, he's really different than people think."

"Maybe," she agreed halfheartedly. "But why haven't you asked me to help?"

"I don't know, Jane. I just hadn't thought about it."

"We used to do everything together, Wendy," she reminded me. "I miss doing things with you. I know that I rather ignored you when I was off the deep end with *you-know-who*, but all that's changed. I was wrong. We can't let that happen again. OK?"

She was right. Jane had been my best friend for years, and it was wrong to let anything hurt that friendship. I nodded *yes*.

"Besides," she went on. "I might be of some help to you. I do have influence in high places, Wendy."

"You do? What are you talking about?"

"You may not be aware of this, my dear," she said in her most imposing voice, "but Ted Carter, *the* Ted Carter, is my uncle."

I gave her a blank stare.

"Oh, Wendy," she cried in disgust. "He does the evening news of Channel Four."

"Oh, *that* Ted Carter! No, I didn't know he was your uncle," I admitted.

"I think you need TV coverage. Politicians can't ignore public interest."

I frowned. "That's what Dad said too, but Mickey doesn't like the idea."

I tried to explain about what Mickey had said and how he felt about being publicized on TV.

"Foolish, foolish pride," Jane concluded. "Well, the offer's still open."

Chapter Thirteen

As usual, I didn't see Mickey until the last period. *A sophomore is a sophomore and a junior is a junior, and never the twain shall meet,* I thought ruefully. If I hadn't had to struggle through algebra, I might never have known him. Still, that was about the only advantage there was to higher mathematics.

After school, he dragged me eagerly toward Crescent Heights. "You won't believe it until you see it, Wendy," Mickey promised. "I came home at lunch. It's almost a miracle."

That was very nearly an understatement. This could not be the same little piece of unkempt, neglected land that it had been a week ago.

It was clean. The grass was neatly mowed, and vibrant splashes of gold marigolds and velvety purple pansies edged the sidewalk. Areas of freshly turned damp earth were carefully marked off with string. The bench, newly painted a sky blue, was in place, and under the one tree sat the picnic table with a big sign propped on it that said "Wet Paint."

I was speechless. The change was beyond my wildest imagination. Now no one could deny that this was a park. It *was* like a miracle!

I stayed rooted to one spot—afraid to step, afraid to touch, afraid it would all disappear. With his arms folded, Mickey waited at the edge of the street.

As we stood there, Nick Marsalas and Tony Carnes, two friends of Mickey's, walked up beside us.

"So, Mick," Tony said, playfully punching him on the arm and throwing his fist up in a fake jab like a prize fighter. "Long time, no see. You been busy?"

Mickey shrugged, but said nothing.

"Hey, Tony," Nick chimed in. "Look at this, we got flowers and strings and all the garbage is gone. It sure looks different. We got us some real class, huh?"

My heart swelled with pride until Tony snickered. It was not a compliment, it was a taunt.

"Yeah, real class. You do all this, Mickey?" Tony asked with scorn.

Mickey shifted his stance and shook his head. "Nah," he said.

"Nah," Nick mimicked him. "Mickey ain't the type to mess around with dirt and junk."

Mickey only stared at him coldly.

"Well, me and Tony was going over to Marty's for a few games of pool. You wanna go? It's been awhile."

I couldn't miss the look of longing that flared in Mickey's eyes and then vanished as he glanced at me. "Not today," he said.

"Suit yourself," Nick replied with a smirky grin. "Just don't forget your old buddies."

Mickey stared at them as they walked away and then viciously kicked at a clod of dirt. "Creeps," he muttered.

Trying to recapture the joy of a few moments past, I turned excitedly to him and cried, "Oh, Mickey, can you believe this?"

"No," he said, his mouth at a funny slant. "It's real crazy."

We weren't talking about the same thing. I eyed him questioningly.

"Me and this dumb park," he said, flinging his hands out wide in a gesture that encompassed the whole area. "Nick was right. Who would believe that Mickey Decker would be sweating some dumb playground?"

"What difference does it make?" I challenged.

He laughed contemptuously. "It's just not my style, you know?"

Slowly I began to understand the truth. It was hard to accept. "Do you really care so much what Tony and Nick think?"

"Maybe," he confessed, turning away from my penetrating gaze.

"You like people to think you're tough and uncaring like those—those creeps?" I flung his words at his back. He clenched his fists at his side before answering.

"Maybe," he mumbled again over his shoulder.

"Well, I've seen the real you, and you're not like that at all," I yelled at him. "You're a fraud, Mickey Decker!"

He jerked his head up and pivoted around. His eyes blazed. "Forget it, Wendy. Don't push me, OK?" he threatened.

"OK," I gave in meekly, stung by his sharp rebuke. A passing cloud blotted out the sunlight. I shivered at the unexpected chill. The lump in my throat was about to explode into tears, and I rummaged through my purse for a tissue, but found the list instead.

I pulled it out and examined it closely, hoping to change the subject. "Well, anyway we've done all we can for now. Or almost everything," I added pointedly.

Mickey's face was as cloudy as the sky. "The press and TV?" he snarled.

"It still could make the difference."

Mickey snatched the paper from my hand, crumpled it, and threw it on the ground. "No publicity!"

I was shaken by his hostility. Instantly, I bent and retrieved the scrap. "Don't litter!" I screamed and stuffed it into my pocket. Then I stomped away from him. I couldn't deal with this Mickey that I had heard about but had never known. How could I have been so blind?

Halfway down the path, he caught up with me and grabbed my arm.

"Wait, Wendy—I'm sorry. Really. Come on, it's going to rain. I'll walk you home." His mood had changed as abruptly as the weather, and the hard look had melted from his face.

Mickey held my hand and we walked the blocks in silence. When we reached my house, we didn't go in, but went around instead to the gazebo. Inside we settled comfortably on the cushioned seat and watched the storm clouds darken the western mountains.

"What happens when it's all over, Wendy?" Mickey asked suddenly.

The question startled me. I twisted around to face him. "We'll either have a park or we'll have a brand new wide, straight street," I jested, deliberately trying to sound light and funny.

He shook his head. "That's not what I mean. I'm talking about you and me. What happens to us when it's over?"

I wasn't sure what to say. Maybe this was his way of saying that he wanted to break it off, that he was tired of me and the park and everything.

I tried to control the quiver in my voice. "What do you want to happen, Mickey?"

"All we've ever done together is talk about the silly piece of ground and worry about it and work on it."

He was right, of course. When you came right down to it, we had never spent any time just talking about ourselves or dating like teenagers are supposed to do.

"I really want to get to know *you*, Wendy." He

squeezed my hand, emphasizing the *you*. "You—without the park or petitions or mayors. I want to know what makes you tick, what makes you laugh, what makes you cry—besides algebra, that is."

I giggled at his joke. "There's not much to know about me," I said shyly. "I'm just your basic, ordinary person. I guess that I laugh and cry over the same things that most people do."

"Where do you come off putting yourself down all the time?" he demanded. "I know plenty of people who would give anything to be as ordinary as you."

He sounded angry again. I wasn't in the mood for any more of his down-and-out speeches, so I agreed with him. "OK, I'm not ordinary, but neither are you," I argued.

"I don't want this to end," he said quietly.

I exhaled a deep breath. "Our friendship?"

His eyes searched mine. "Isn't it anything more than that?"

My heart skipped several beats before I answered. "Maybe. I think it could be in time."

We sat in the gazebo for a long time after that, not saying anything, not doing anything, until Mickey spoke again.

"I didn't know how you felt," he explained. "I was afraid—"

I wanted to interrupt him, but he laid his finger on my mouth. "You be quiet and listen. It isn't easy for me to say the things I need to say to you." Hesitantly he began again. "I was afraid you would realize that we are different. When the park's torn up, you'll understand what I'm trying to say. Then maybe you won't care so much about me."

Looking at his strong arms, feeling that strength close to me, I could not imagine him being afraid of anything. But I knew that there are things to fear from deep inside, and I knew that there is only One who can help us overcome that kind of fear.

"Don't think so little of me, Mickey," I begged. "I'm not like that. I don't care where you live or how much money you've got. I only care about you. And what do you mean 'when the park's torn up'?" I was suddenly angry. "They wouldn't do that. Not after all the work we've done."

He laughed. "Oh, they not only can, they will."

I refused to let him discourage me. "Don't be such a pessimist."

"Not a pessimist, Wendy," he assured me. "A realist. And you're a dreamer. If the people in your neighborhood wanted a park, they'd get a park. But who cares about some poor kids in Crescent Heights?"

I thought of myself and how everything seemed to come naturally to Cammie and Mom and Dad and how I had to try so hard. It was the same thing. I knew how he felt. I put my hand over his.

"So life's not fair," I said. "So what? This time I just know that everything's going to come out all right. It has to."

"I hope you're right, Wendy. I'm sorry about before—about yelling at you. I know you're probably right about publicity. But you don't understand. Sometimes—sometimes, pride is all you've got."

"No, Mickey, you're wrong. You've got me, and . . ." I swallowed hard. "You've got Jesus if you'd just believe that."

He frowned again. "Don't get off on that religious stuff with me again, Wendy. Not now."

What could I say? I was afraid to chance his anger again. After he left, I sat in the gazebo alone for a long time and prayed for him to forget his pride and come to Jesus.

In the kitchen Dad was humming loudly as he stirred

a big pot of soup. I tiptoed up behind him and gave him a big hug around his middle.

"Wendy, you saw the park?"

"It's unbelievable, Dad. How did you do it?"

"I didn't do it all," he replied with modesty. "Mrs. Decker and the Websters worked over there all morning. The picnic table adds just the right touch, and don't the flowers look good?"

I nodded and tried to smile. I guess I didn't try hard enough. Dad knew immediately that something was wrong. He laid down his big spoon and turned to me. "What's the matter, Wendy?" he asked.

I sighed. "I never seem to do anything right, Dad." I told him about everything that had happened at the park. "But the worst part," I said, "is that I wanted to talk to Mickey about Jesus, and he totally turned me off. He's so stubborn!"

Dad smiled sympathetically. "You'll have another chance, Wendy. And don't forget, the way we live is a witness too. Don't rush him."

That made me feel better. Somehow Dad always knew the right answer.

He dished up a spoonful of soup and offered it to me. "Watch out, it's hot!" he warned.

Grimacing, I cautiously sipped the soup and nodded my approval. Even cream of alfalfa sprouts would have tasted good right then.

"Nothing like soup on a gray day," Dad said brightly.

While we shared sips of the steaming liquid, I told Dad about Jane's uncle and he explained that he had taken some "after" pictures and called his friend John Anderson again.

"So what's next?" I asked impatiently.

"We'll just have to wait now. It looks like the Lord is going to help out. Some rain is just what we need for the new grass." Then he added, "We're only commanded to sow the seed, Wendy. We can't make it grow." I knew he wasn't talking about grass.

"You're doing a fine thing, Wendy."

I smiled at his compliment, but shrugged it off. "We wouldn't have gotten anywhere without you."

"Oh, I don't know about that. Mickey's not the only stubborn one." He grinned at me and then went into the pantry.

Rejoicing again at the miracle of the park, I hardly heard the back door open and close. The next thing I knew, Cammie was grasping my arm.

Her appearance alarmed me. The darkness of her eyes was the only color on her face. Her mouth twitched as she whispered, "I've got to talk to you."

Then she almost ran from the kitchen. Immediately I followed her up the stairs and into my room. She quickly closed the door behind us and leaned heavily on it.

"Read this," she commanded and shoved a crumpled piece of paper toward me.

Chapter Fourteen

I unfolded the paper and studied the message scrawled in bright colored crayon lettering: *I have Crystal. Will contact you later with an interesting proposition.*

I read the words twice before looking in panic at Cammie.

Her hands shook as she took the paper from me and crammed it into her jacket pocket.

"Wendy, it's unreal. I was at the gallery. Mom had to run some errands and asked me to come in and close up the shop for her. I—" She spoke in gasping breaths.

"Slow down," I warned.

She closed her eyes and took several deep breaths. Then she sat down on the edge of the rocker. "OK. This young boy came in the shop. I was at the counter. He asked if I was Mrs. Thomsen. Then he just stuck this out at me." She pulled the note from her pocket and held it out. "He waved it in my face and threw it on the counter. Then he turned around and left before I could read it."

I tried to picture the scene and to imagine Cammie's startled expression.

"I didn't know what to do at first; then I followed him out to the street and stopped him. I asked him why he called me Mrs. Thomsen. He didn't say anything. Oh,

Wendy, he just held out his hand and showed me this!"

Cammie unclenched her fist. I gasped. In the palm of her hand was the other half of the golden locket! Picking it up, I gazed in astonishment at the photograph there.

"Mom?" I choked in a half whisper. The picture was undeniably our mother when she was young. "No wonder he thought you were—"

Cammie nodded her head. "I tried to ask him who had given him the locket, but he dropped it and ran away. I chased him through the bookstore next door and toward the back exit."

"And you lost him in the alley?" It was a logical guess, but she shook her head jerkily.

"Someone stopped me. A man . . . he grabbed my arm and spun me around. I'll never forget that face." She shuddered. "Those bushy eyebrows, and beady little eyes, that bald head—"

"Carter Crenshaw?" I cried in amazement.

"I think so. I've only seen him that one time he came here and that was from a distance."

"What did he say to you?"

"Oh, I don't know." She gnawed at her lip. "I wasn't paying much attention. I only wanted to get away from him. But I do remember one strange thing—"

"Which was?" I prompted.

"He knew my name. He called me Miss Thomsen."

She caught my puzzled expression, and her voice grew icily calm as she answered me. "Wendy, how did he know who I was?"

Her eyes darted to the locket.

"He's never seen me before."

A chill ran down my spine. With the frightening note in one hand and the locket in the other, Cammie fell back against the chair. I slumped on the bed.

"What do we do now?" I asked.

Cammie moaned. "We have to tell Mom."

A knock startled both of us. Cammie quickly shoved the paper and the gold heart into her pocket once more. I stepped to the door. It was Dad.

"Your mother's home," he said. "She's waiting in the family room." Even from the doorway, there was no chance he could overlook Cammie's distraught condition. Quickly he went to her and knelt beside the chair.

"Cammie, what on earth—?" he questioned. "Are you ill?"

She shook her head. Then reaching into her pocket, she produced the note. "Dad, the portrait's gone. I know we should have said something sooner, but—"

Mom's clear voice rang out from the bottom of the stairs. "Rob, are you coming?"

Dad looked intently at the scrap of paper and then at both of us.

"I've been expecting something like this. Don't say anything to your mother," he cautioned. "I'll take care of it."

"But, Dad, do you know who—?" I stammered.

"I'm afraid so," he answered tersely and left the room.

There was a storm brewing in more ways than one as we gathered downstairs. My feelings matched the oppressive atmosphere. I watched Mom take her accustomed place on the sofa. The deep lilac of her blouse emphasized the dark circles under her eyes. A throb of concern and fear swept over me. Someone was threatening my mother. But who?

The clues all pointed in only one direction, and, like Cammie, I didn't want to accept that. Why Sean, or anyone else, would want to hurt my mother was beyond my imagination.

Dad remained as calm as ever. Mechanically he passed out small glasses of chilled tomato juice, then sat on the edge of the sofa by Mom and enthusiastically recounted his day's activities.

I watched Mom nervously. The corners of her mouth tightened. I knew she wasn't as excited about the park as Dad and I, but the depth of her resentment staggered me.

Setting her glass of untasted juice firmly on the end table, she frowned at Dad.

"You spent the entire day working on that—that place?" she demanded. "Instead of your book?"

Dad's eyebrows furrowed together as he nodded yes.

"I can't understand what's happening to this family," Mom cried.

I shivered. The air was suddenly cooler, and a slight breeze picked at the sheer white window curtains.

I sneaked a look at Cammie, who very deliberately licked a smear of red juice from her upper lip, shrugged her shoulders, and looked away.

Mom's accusations continued. "Robert, aren't you going to finish your book? And Cammie . . . you've quit practicing. The audition is next month."

I was next. I cringed inwardly.

"And Wendy spends all her time with that Decker boy."

A distant rumble of thunder punctuated her speech.

Dad didn't answer, but his eyes, ablaze with disbelief, said more than words could. Cammie's mouth flew open to protest, then shut tightly as a closer, louder peal of thunder drowned out whatever she had started to say.

I blinked back angry tears, but held my silence, praying for a gentle answer and understanding heart. Through the billowing curtains, I focused my attention on the swiftly moving rain clouds and far-away flashes of lightning.

The wind increased to sharp gusts. Except for its whining whistle, no sound broke the agonizing stillness.

Finally Dad took a deep breath and answered her in a firm voice. "Joanna, you're being too harsh."

Mom jerked her head up. Her dark eyes flashed angrily, but Dad's upraised hand stifled any quick reply. "I don't have to make excuses for what I do. The book will be finished on time. There's no need to worry."

Dad's voice had a stern, reproving tone to it. I felt sorry for Mom.

"I think," he continued evenly, "it would be better if you discussed your feelings in a rational way, a more Christian way, instead of like this."

My mother's shoulders slumped wearily. Her eyes filled with tears as she shook her head. "Oh, Rob, Cammie, Wendy. I've done it again! That was an unforgivable outburst. I'm so ashamed." Her face dropped into her hands, and Dad reached out to lovingly put his arm around her. "Maybe it's this weather," she mumbled. "I hate storms."

Dad refused to change the subject. "There's something else, isn't there, Jo?" he asked, using his pet name for her. "Are there problems at the gallery? You haven't said much about it lately."

That was true. Suddenly feeling guilty, I wondered if all of us had been too busy to pay any attention to her.

She sighed. "Not really, except that Sean hasn't been getting his work ready for the show as quickly as I had hoped. There's so much to do, advertisements, invitations. It's just not coming together as well as I wanted."

"What can we do to help?" Dad inquired sympathetically.

The quality of Mom's voice changed, becoming peevish. "Maybe if Sean didn't spend so much time with you and Cammie, he could spend more time on his show." She looked pointedly at each of them, and added, "And you could spend more time on your audition, Cammie. You haven't changed your mind, have you?"

Cammie's back stiffened and her face flushed. She looked desperately at Dad. "I don't know, Mom," she answered, staring past her. "It doesn't seem as important to me as it once did."

I can't describe Mom's face. It was as though someone had slapped her. She instantly regained her composure, but her voice, a strained whisper, betrayed her. "It's been my dream for so long."

Cammie twisted her head and looked sadly in Mom's direction. "I know that, Mom. I'm just not sure that it's my dream anymore."

"You're so talented. You can't let that go to waste." She turned helplessly toward Dad, then back to Cammie. "It's Sean, isn't it?"

Before Cammie could answer, lightning tore the skies apart! I held my breath and automatically counted the seconds, computing the distance of the storm. But there was no interval between light and noise as wave after wave of brilliance signaled the next crashing rumble. Hail came in staccato beats, the wind ripped at the curtains, and the lights paled and died.

"Quickly," Dad shouted. "Check the doors and windows!"

Each of us scurried from the room. Our motions, illuminated by the rapid flashes of lightning, seemed quick and exaggerated like the flickering movements of a silent movie.

I raced upstairs, Dad headed for the kitchen, Mom went to her studio, and Cammie ran to the living room. As suddenly as it had begun, the storm diminished in intensity and the howling wind became a whisper. The lights flicked on, and it was strangely quiet. I thought of the storm on the lake and Jesus' command, "Peace, be still." But this was only momentary.

Mom's urgent voice pierced the silence. "Rob! Where are you?"

Something was very wrong. She sounded hysterical.

I skipped down the steps two at a time. Dad ran from the kitchen. Cammie stopped in the entrance of the living room and eyed me questioningly.

Then Mom appeared from the direction of her studio. Her hair was disheveled and her face pale. Rain drops spotted her brightly colored blouse.

"Rob?" Her voice quivered.

"Here, Joanna, what—?"

"Rob!" she gasped. "The portrait . . . the portrait . . . it's gone!"

Cammie stood frozen in the living room doorway. My foot hung midway between two steps. Dad reached out quickly and took both of Mom's hands in his.

"Calm down," he directed. "Take a deep breath."

Holding tightly to his hands, she took several ragged breaths. Then she turned panic-stricken eyes to him. "It's gone, Rob. For some reason the window in the storage room was open. It's never open, but it was tonight. I went in to check the window, and the easel's empty."

When he didn't move, she gestured impatiently with her head toward the hallway. "Go look for yourself."

Dad tried to reassure her. "Maybe someone moved it by mistake. You know Cammie showed Sean around your studio the other day. Perhaps they moved it to the other room."

Glancing at Cammie, Mom responded with unexpected calm. "I remember that, but the painting wasn't moved to the other room. It's been stolen."

"Yes," Dad said as he released her hands and moved toward the telephone in the hall.

But Mom was quicker and put her hand on his arm,

holding him back. "What are you doing, Rob?"

"I'm calling the police."

"No." She shook her head. "We can't do that. No police."

Dad insisted. "Joanna, we have to." He took a deep breath. "Don't you see? It's gone far enough. Read this."

Mom's hands shook as she scanned the short note. "You already knew?"

"Yes," he said again.

She stared at him, her face ashen but emotionless. "No police, Rob, please," she begged.

Dad nodded finally. He understood something that I did not. With his assistance, Mom climbed the stairs, the paper still clasped tightly in her hand.

Cammie looked at me strangely. Her mouth opened to speak, but no sounds came. The ring of the telephone broke the awesome silence.

I answered it. Through the crackling static of the electrical storm, it was difficult to hear the garbled words before the phone went dead. But it was impossible not to recognize the voice.

I faced Cammie. "It was Sean."

"What did he—"

One last muted clap of thunder drowning out her words signaled that the rain had begun.

With trembling hands, I replaced the receiver. "I'm not sure. It was hard to hear . . ." My voice quivered. "I think he asked if Mom had gotten his message."

Chapter Fifteen

I awakened the next morning to a misty gray dawn. Snuggling deep under the covers, I tried to capture a few more moments of sleep, but something gnawed at my subconscious. My eyes flew open. The note . . . the phone call . . . Mom. Oh, Mom! With a breaking heart, I recalled the panic in her eyes, the desperation in her voice.

Then I remembered Dad's calming promise. "I'll take care of it." And the knowing look on his face last night. There was nothing I could do, nothing Cammie could do, but trust Dad . . . and God.

My thoughts seesawed from Mickey to the park, from Cammie to Mom, until finally, throwing the covers aside, I headed for the shower. At last the relaxing spray eased some of the tension in my body and mind.

I psyched myself up to expect only the best from this day. After dressing in jeans and adding a bright red sweater for a defiant dash of color, I skipped down the stairs toward the kitchen.

I met Dad coming up. "Careful, Wendy," he warned. He was balancing a tray of fluffy scrambled eggs, golden juice, and steamy black coffee. "I thought your mother deserved a little *T.L.C.* this morning," he explained. "She didn't sleep well last night."

I nodded sympathetically. Poor Mom. She must have been really depressed. I decided to go in and see her before I left for school.

Cammie sat at the breakfast table, nursing a mug of rich hot chocolate, her eyes glued to the small portable TV on the kitchen counter.

"Hi, Cammie—"

"Sh-h-h," she silenced me. "Listen to the news."

"—knocked out power lines," the reporter was saying. "Irrigation canals and creeks are filled to capacity. The rain is expected to continue for several days, and a bulletin has been issued for a flash flood watch. And this note just in—Mountain Falls High School has canceled classes for the day due to a power outage in that area. Repeat: No school today at Mountain Falls High."

"No school?" I repeated incredulously. A whole day of unearned freedom? A delicious day for curling up with a good book or visiting with Jane or spending some time with Mickey.

My thoughts came to a dead halt. Crescent Heights was only a short distance from the high school. If the storm had been that severe in that area, what about the park? I grabbed for the telephone and dialed Mickey's number. A recording increased my fears. The telephone lines were down. I had to get over there and see for myself.

"Tell Dad I had to go out," I yelled at Cammie as I rushed from the room. I jerked my yellow rain jacket from the hall closet, hastily slipped it on, and pulled the hood tightly about my head.

Outside the wind had faded to an imitation of last night's fury, but it pelted light drops of rain in my face as I trudged down the street. Anxious glances at broken tree limbs and leaves strewn across neighboring yards increased my apprehension and my speed. Heedlessly I plunged through small muddy rivers washing across the sidewalk. My water-soaked sneakers squished as I reached Fourth Street, my breath coming in short gasps.

I entered the path, then stopped, and gazed with dismay. A sick feeling welled up in me. With tears blurring the scene, I could only stare mutely at the devastation. Dizzily I reached out to the little tree for support. An arm clutched my waist, steadying me. I raised my eyes and stared into Mickey's.

"Disaster area, Wendy," he scoffed. "It's gone."

I shook my head unbelievingly and buried my face against his damp jacket. "It's only a bad dream," I wailed, clinging to him.

He laughed. "I knew you were a dreamer. Well, wake up, Wendy, and look around. This is for real."

I lifted my head, took a deep breath, and did as he commanded.

The picnic table was overturned. Floating in a puddle of muddy water the "Wet Paint" sign was now illegible. The wind-whipped marigolds and pansies hung lifelessly from broken stems. Small crevices riddled the newly planted areas allowing the grass seed to wash in rivulets to the street. Only the old bench remained bravely upright, but its fresh coat of paint was chipped and pitted by the hail.

"We can fix it," I insisted. "As soon as the rain stops, when it dries up, we'll start over. We'll—"

"Give it up, Wendy," Mickey interjected, holding me at arms' length and forcing me to look at him. "We've lost."

I stared into his face. Raindrops hung tenaciously to his eyelashes. The dampness curled his black hair, making tendrils around his forehead. He was wrong. He had to be wrong.

"Just like that?" I cried. "Just throw it all away, just

pretend that it never happened?"

"It was a dumb idea from the beginning," he retorted. "Nobody cares about this jerky place!"

"I do!" I screamed. Then something he had said before surfaced in my mind. With new hope, I challenged him. "You told me once you were a survivor."

His hands dropped to his sides. A look of pain clouded his eyes. "The first lesson in survival is knowing when to quit," he said without emotion.

Stuffing his hands into his windbreaker pockets, he stalked away.

"Mickey, wait!" I pleaded, breaking into a trot after him.

"No, Wendy," a deep voice called from behind me. "Let him go."

Whirling around, I saw my father walking toward me. I had not even noticed the station wagon pull up on the far side of the park.

I went to him. A few drops of rain mingled with the tears on my cheeks. Dad put his arm around my shoulder and let me sob. "We've done the best we can, Wendy," he said, patting me consolingly.

Startled, I looked up at him. "Does this mean that you've given up too?" I demanded, rubbing my fist savagely across my eyes.

He shook his head. "Not at all. We still have the pictures, and the mayor called after you left. They've agreed to put the park on the agenda for the commissioners' meeting Monday night. He and John Anderson are coming by this weekend to look."

"Look at what?" I asked. "There's nothing left."

Dad shrugged. "Then we'll just have to hope for the best and do some earnest praying."

I didn't feel like praying. I was too angry. I felt like God had let me down. "Why did God do this?" I asked with bitterness. "Is He mad at me? Have I done something wrong? Is it because I haven't tried hard enough to tell Mickey about Jesus?"

Dad cupped my chin in his hand. "No, no, Wendy. You mustn't feel that way." He took out his handkerchief and mopped off the splintery bench. "Come, sit down with me," he urged.

"No," I protested, shaking my head vigorously. "I don't want to stay here. I don't want to look at it anymore."

"Refusing to face our problems won't make them go away," Dad cautioned. Firmly, but gently too, he pulled me down beside him. I glared stonily at gray clouds and sniffled back the last of my tears.

"Wendy, we weren't promised that there would be no rain, only that there would be a rainbow. You can't blame the Lord. Things just happen sometimes."

"But why do they always happen to me?" I moaned.

Dad squeezed my hand. "It's not just you, dear girl. Everyone has a share of bad times."

I was sure he was thinking of Mom.

Suddenly ashamed of myself, I cried, "What about Mom? What do we do about her?"

Worry tightened the corners of his mouth, but his words were brave. "There's nothing you can do, Wendy, but wait. Your mother is a strong person. You've got to trust me to handle it. It'll all work out. Believe me."

Dad made it sound so right. I forced a halfhearted grin.

As we walked toward the car, I tried to believe him, but doubt rampaged within me. I sank into a deep huddle in the front seat. As we drove away, I focused my attention on the steady rhythm of the windshield wipers and refused to look back at Crescent Heights.

Chapter Sixteen

Mom spent most of the day in her room. She didn't even come down for lunch. "Napping," Dad explained.

Cammie and I exchanged worried, mystified looks but said nothing.

By that evening, I could stand it no longer. After dinner, I barged into Cammie's room without knocking. She whirled around to face me, but not before slamming shut the lid of the jewelry box on her dressing table.

"Wendy, good grief!" she exclaimed. "I thought maybe it was Mom." She sighed with relief.

"The locket?"

"I put it in here. I keep staring at it, trying to understand . . ."

She opened the box, extracted the gold trinket, and held it toward me. It caught the light and blazed like a momentary star. Where did this golden link fit into the mysterious chain that bound us all?

I stared at the still image of my mother, the black hair and the dark eyes, which repeated itself in the face of my sister.

"Do you think Crystal was *her* sister?"

"It's possible," Cammie mused. "But they're so different, like day and night. Besides, that would mean . . . that would make Sean . . ."

"Our cousin?"

Cammie laughed nervously. "He can't be," she said, but her voice sounded hollow as she added, "Not that I care anymore."

I watched her, surprised by her admission but afraid to pry.

She sat down at the dresser and announced calmly, "He's left town, Wendy. I know you and Dad suspect Sean, but I—" Her voice cracked. "I didn't want to believe it. I called him. His landlady told me he has gone to Chicago."

"Chicago?" I echoed, raising my head. I squeezed my eyes shut. Something in the back of my mind begged to be remembered. "That's in Illinois."

"OK. You get an *A* in geography!" Cammie snapped. Turning around, she started brushing her dark hair vigorously.

"The license plate on the yellow VW was from Illinois," I mumbled.

"Not Carter Crenshaw again?"

I nodded. With her back to me, Cammie scrutinized my reflection in her mirror. "So what?" she said. "It's only a coincidence."

"It has to be," I conceded.

A wet weekend dragged by. Mickey called and briefly informed me that he had a chance to work and would see me on Monday.

Cammie spent most of her time practicing. Mom stayed pretty much to herself. Nothing more was said about the missing painting or the crayon-scribbled message. Dad invented zucchini wheat germ brownies (yuk!), and Sydney Carton was beheaded in my book.

I tried not to think too much about the park.

Jane called and invited me over, but I begged off. I didn't have to see her to know what she would say: "You know, Wendy, sometimes life rains on our parade!"

I didn't need philosophical puns. I needed a strategy. But my brain was as dry as the outside world was wet.

Dad asked if Mickey and I would like to go to the town meeting with him on Monday night. I didn't know if I really wanted to or not. I was scared. As long as it was just something ahead, something we could anticipate, then we were safe. But once the meeting became a reality, and we actually faced the fact and heard it talked about and voted on, then it became a threat. It was like Christmas. The best part is waiting for it and hoping that you get that one thing you've always wanted. Then when it happens, there's always kind of a letdown.

Only a handful of people were at the meeting. Three men and a woman sat at the front of the room at a long table with papers spread out in front of them and some sound equipment so that everyone could hear what was said.

We waited for nearly an hour while they went over other things on the agenda. Evidently Crescent Heights was not a high priority item.

Finally it was our turn. The mayor explained to the others about the situation. He also explained about the plans for Fourth Street. On a map of the city, he pointed out exactly where the park was. After very little discussion, one of the men suggested that they put it to a vote.

It just didn't seem fair to me to have it all over and done with so soon. Then Mayor Dennison asked if anyone else had anything to add before the vote was called for.

Dad raised his hand and was recognized. "Mr. Dennison, before you make up your minds, I would like you to see these photographs." He took the pictures up to the table and spread them out.

"I'd like to say," Dad continued, "that the people of Crescent Heights have worked very hard to make this area into a place where their children can play and they can visit and relax. There is no other park anywhere near that neighborhood. If it's destroyed, the children will have no playground. In addition to that, by widening Fourth Street you will increase the traffic hazards for that neighborhood. In my opinion, it would serve a better purpose to save the park and try some other way to do something about the street."

"Do you also have some suggestion about that, Dr. Thomsen?" the lady commissioner asked.

Dad reluctantly admitted that he did not.

"Don't you realize that a new shopping mall is being built here?" Commissioner Green asked. He pointed to a place on the map. "We promised the contractors that something would be done about increasing the flow of traffic in that area so people could have easier access to the shopping center."

So that's what it was all about! I glanced uneasily at Mickey. A sullen frown played at his mouth.

"And big business is more important than the residents of Crescent Heights?" Dad asked with a tone of hostility.

"Big business pays big taxes, Dr. Thomsen," the gentleman responded unsympathetically. "I don't need to remind you that the city needs additional revenue for other improvements. Besides, I drove by there myself Saturday. That place is nothing but a mudhole and an eyesore. I think it would be a definite improvement to get rid of it once and for all!" He leaned back in his chair as though the matter were settled.

Next to me, I could feel Mickey stiffen. His head shot up and he glared angrily at the commissioners. Once again, Dad tried to persuade them. He told how hard we had worked and pointed to the pictures again. He tried to convince them that with drier weather, it could all be done again. Dad's eloquent appeal fell on deaf ears.

I could see the look of defeat in Mickey's eyes even before the vote. Three no's and one yes. The lady commissioner was the only one who agreed with us that the park should stay. The work would begin as scheduled on Friday.

It was so unfair! I think Dad felt even worse than I did. Mickey wouldn't look at me as we left the building. Nor did he say anything as we drove home. It was too dark to see his face, but I didn't need to. He held my hand tightly, too tightly, and his harsh grasp told me what he felt.

"I'm sorry, Mickey," Dad apologized as he stopped in front of the Deckers' home. "I don't know what else we could have done."

"It doesn't matter," Mickey answered. He got out of the car and went into his house before anything else was said.

"He's very disappointed, Wendy. I feel sorry for him," Dad commented.

I didn't know if he really was disappointed. He never did believe it would happen. Not like I did.

We drove home in silence. As we walked into the house, I looked up at Dad. "Is this the absolute end? Isn't there anything else we can do?"

Dad shook his head. "I can't think of anything, Wendy. Can you?"

Not yet, but three days were left for me to think about it.

It wasn't very late. Mom was still sitting in the family room when we walked in. Cammie was with her.

"Well," she asked, "how did it go?" Surely she could tell by the look on my face.

Dad answered her. "We lost. They begin tearing up the park on Friday."

I hoped I was mistaken, but I thought I saw a look of relief brighten Mom's face. I wasn't wrong.

"I'm sorry, Rob, but I am glad that that's all over and done with. Now maybe we can get back to normal."

Her words hurt me more than I had thought possible.

"What do you mean it's over and done with?" I asked. It was wrong to antagonize her. It was the last thing she needed, but I couldn't stop myself.

She looked straight at me. "Now you can quit spending so much time with Mickey in that dreadful neighborhood."

"Mom, Mickey happens to be a very good friend of mine," I cried, "and I like that neighborhood and I'm sorry, but it isn't the end—at least not the end of my friendship with him or with Crescent Heights."

"Wendy, you can't be serious." The tone of her voice had not changed. She remained calm in spite of my outburst. "You know I've never been happy about what you were doing. I should have tried to stop you. I knew it would come to this. But now it's over, finished. You lost. Don't you understand?"

"No, I don't understand," I said defiantly. "Or maybe I do. You don't really care, do you?"

"Wendy, don't—!" Dad's sharp exclamation silenced my words.

I had never spoken to my mother like that before. I blushed red with shame before the words were even out, but it was too late.

I saw her flinch and take a deep breath. Then she spoke quietly. "Do you really think that? Do you really believe that I don't care about you or even the park?"

I looked helplessly at Dad. "I don't know what I think."

Mom turned to face my sister. "And, Cammie, do you also believe that I don't care about *you* because I have insisted on the audition?" It was not a question to be answered.

"It's not true," Mom said evenly. She closed her eyes and shook her head. "I care so much. I knew you couldn't win in Crescent Heights. You *don't* understand, do you?" She looked imploringly from Cammie to me. "I only wanted to save you both from heartbreak. I failed, didn't I?"

Dad sat down beside her on the sofa and took her hands in his. He looked at her in a gentle, noncondemning way.

"Not failed, Joanna, not that," he said.

Mom looked suddenly small and tired, but her chin jutted out bravely as she agreed with him. "No, *deceived* would be a better choice of words. Maybe it's time we got it all out in the open. It's too late now for half truths."

"You're right, Jo. We have to get things straightened out now. Cammie," he said without moving his gaze from Mom, "I want you to phone Sean. Ask him to come over, and—" he paused and gripped Mom's hands more tightly. "Tell him to bring the painting."

Chapter Seventeen

Mom exhaled a low moan. Her back went rigid. "No, Rob, I don't want him in this house."

Cammie looked questioningly from one to the other. "But he left town."

Dad insisted, "Now, Cammie."

We sat like frozen statues. No one moved. No one spoke. It seemed like hours before Cammie returned and said, "He'll be here in a few minutes."

Mom struggled to rise from the sofa. "Not this way," she begged.

Dad held her back. "Jo, it's the only way. Please trust me."

"I do, Rob," Mom said quietly, sinking back. "You're right. We have to get this behind us so that we can go on living."

Dad relaxed his hold and smiled. "Good. Now while we're waiting I'll put on a pot of coffee."

Time stood still. Dad left to go to the kitchen. Cammie retreated to the window seat, hugged a cushion close to her, and gazed into the darkness outside. Mom stared straight ahead, her hands knit together in her lap. Her face was pale and expressionless like a piece of chiseled marble.

This was my family. I looked from one to the other with love. Somehow I knew, and dreaded knowing, that nothing would ever be the same. I prayed earnestly that we would be the better for it.

I jumped when the doorbell sounded, but Mom did not react. Dad set his coffee cup down and touched her arm as if to say *it's all right*. Then he motioned for me to answer the door.

Sean, in jeans and a gravy sweat shirt, walked into the room. Glancing first at Mom and then at Cammie, he hesitated for a moment before leaning a brown paper-wrapped parcel against the fireplace hearth.

Mom spoke first. "Why? Why did you come here—bringing a ghost into my house?" Reproach was in her voice.

"The ghost was your creation, Mrs. Thomsen," Sean replied quietly.

"Yes," Mom admitted in a husky whisper. She looked at Dad once more with a pleading expression. Again he reached out and took her hand.

"Tell them."

Slowly at first, but without faltering, Mom related the story.

"Sean's mother and I were sisters. Not blood sisters—her mother and my father married when we were young children. We grew up together. It was a strange coincidence that we both had a talent for art. Then the chance came for us to study in Paris. Both of us won scholarships. I remember how excited we were—the plans we made, the dreams we dreamed."

She stopped and sighed. "Dear Crystal. But Papa was ill, very ill. Someone had to stay. Someone had to care for him. I should have been the one. He was my real father, but she insisted that I go. She was younger, she said. She would have time."

"I promised to return in six months, and she would have her chance, but—"

"You never went back," Sean murmured.

Mom closed her eyes tightly. "No, I never went back. It was so wonderful, the school and the teachers. It was all that we had hoped for. I thought he couldn't live forever. She would still have her opportunity. He lived for two long years. Crystal, she . . . wouldn't, couldn't leave him.

"Then it was too late. The scholarship had elapsed. It was before I met Robert, before he taught me about God's love." She turned to Dad. "You tried to get me to see her, to ask her forgiveness, but I was ashamed, so ashamed.

"Later she married, and there was Sean. When she died so young, I—" She stopped abruptly.

"You stopped painting," Sean completed her sentence.

"Yes."

"It was a waste, Mrs. Thomsen."

Mom shook her head. "There was no more beauty, no depth to what I did. The last thing I tried . . ." She looked toward the still-covered package. "When you walked into the gallery that first day, I knew. There was no mistaking who you were. But I thought you didn't know me. I thought I could make it all up to you. Then after Cammie showed you the painting, I knew you had to know, and I was frightened. Why *did* you come?" There was no reproach now.

"To try to help you," he answered simply.

"But why—" I stammered. "Why did you take the painting?"

My words hung in the air. Sean's eyes widened in surprise as he looked from Mom to me. "But I didn't. *I* didn't take the portrait." He turned to Dad with a puzzled expression. "I thought you knew."

Cammie looked at me strangely, and then spoke for the first time. "Then who?"

"Carter Crenshaw," Dad said flatly.

My mouth dropped open. "The real estate agent?" I cried.

"No, Wendy, an art critic," Mom explained. "A has-been art critic."

"Who loved my mother and despised yours," Sean added.

"He always had a fascination for Crystal. He always blamed me for . . . for . . ." Mom covered her face with her hands. "He was right."

Slowly the puzzle pieces dropped into place. Crenshaw had known my mother and her sister from the beginning, and he had kept track through the years. Both he and Sean lived in Chicago. He had come to Sean hoping to enlist him in the conspiracy.

"He actually thought I would be willing to steal from you. He thought I had that much hate in my heart. I followed him here. I thought I could stop him."

Then Sean explained why. "It was for revenge mostly. And also for ransom. He thought Dr. Thomsen would pay dearly to get the painting back. He's in desperate need of money."

"Poor, poor Carter," Mom murmured.

"He won't bother you now," Sean continued. "I threatened to tell the police if he ever tried to pull something like this again."

"But the locket?" Cammie questioned.

Sean's eyes misted over. "My mother's half. He stole that too. Long ago."

One final link remained to the chain of puzzles. "But I don't understand about the message."

"It was Crenshaw who sent it, of course." Both Cammie and I turned to Father with looks of astonishment.

"You knew that all along?" she asked.

"Yes, so did your mother."

"You mean," Cammie went on, "you never suspected Sean?"

Dad shook his head.

"But on the phone, the night of the storm," I insisted. "Sean said . . . he asked if Mom had received his message."

"No, Wendy, I asked if you would give her a message, but then the connection went dead. I wanted to tell her that I had gone to Chicago. I thought she would understand why."

Mom's face had returned to its natural color. She was almost smiling now as she whispered, "Thank you for rescuing the portrait, Sean."

"There's just one thing," he said slowly. "I would like to hang it at the show with the rest of my work. You see, it's mine now." Then he reached out and tore the wrappings away.

I held my breath. My attention was riveted to the canvas. The portrait was complete. With brilliant hues, with masterful strokes, he had brought the young girl to life.

Mom's eyes filled with tears. "Crystal," she whispered. "Can you forgive me?"

"She did, a long time ago," Sean answered. "She always loved you."

Mom sighed. "If only I could forgive myself. But you understand now, don't you, Cammie, why you mustn't let your talent go to waste? I wasted Crystal's and mine, but I didn't want that to happen to you.

"And dear Wendy, how awful you think I am, not caring about your park. But it's not like that. You see, I grew up in Crescent Heights. It was *my* neighborhood."

My eyes asked the question. She shook her head. "Not here. Every city has a Crescent Heights." She turned away from the sad memories. "I only wanted to protect you both from the pain."

"I've made too many mistakes, but I never want to hurt you, not any of you." She looked pleadingly at Cammie, at me, and, lastly, at Sean.

Slowly, understanding replaced my disbelief. I felt so sad for my mother that I ached with the hurt.

"It's OK, Mom," Cammie said softly. Then in the same instant, we moved toward her. Our arms went around her and each other. "It's OK, Mom," Cammie repeated in a choked voice. "We love you."

Sean quietly slipped away and left us alone.

Chapter Eighteen

So much had happened that night that it was impossible to sleep. Like leaves blowing in the wind, my thoughts raced back and forth, up and down.

We had lost the park. Somehow I had never thought it would end so quickly, so easily. All the time and love we had put into it had been ignored—cast aside like nothing.

And my mother—what had we done to her? It seemed so simple when she had explained it. But it is not a simple thing to bare one's soul. There was no sense of victory.

And what about Mickey? He had never really expected it to happen, and he had been right. Was he the realist and I the dreamer? Could we go on now? Was there anything left for us?

Something in me refused to admit defeat. There must be another route we could take, some higher court we could appeal to.

"Dad, who are the commissioners and the mayor answerable to?" I asked the next morning at breakfast as I toyed with my cereal.

"I don't know exactly what you mean, Wendy."

I put my spoon down. "Do they always have the final say about what goes in this town? Is there someone else that's higher, like the supreme court or something?"

"This isn't a law case with appeals, you know," he said, still in the dark.

"I know that, but isn't there someone or somewhere that we can go to?" I demanded. "How do they get their authority?"

"They're elected. The people vote for them," he answered.

"That's it, then," I said enthusiastically. Suddenly it seemed very clear to me.

"What's *it*?" Cammie asked. She had been following the conversation. "What in the world are you getting at?"

"The people, the voters, the public. We were wrong, Dad. Mickey was wrong, and I was wrong to agree with him. We *should* have gotten some publicity. We should have let the TV and papers in on this."

"I agree, Wendy," Dad said. "Maybe I should have forced the issue. But Mickey had to be considered too."

"It's still not too late," I insisted, rising from the table. "There are still three days before the work begins. Jane promised that she would talk to Ted Carter. It just can't be too late, Dad."

He shook his head. "There isn't another meeting for two weeks. Even if there were some public sympathy, I don't think it would do any good now."

I started toward the door. "Where are you going, Wendy?" Mom asked. "You haven't eaten your breakfast."

I turned back and grinned. "To look for the rainbow," I replied as I dashed out the door to catch the bus.

At lunchtime, Jane called her uncle at the TV station.

She had agreed to do this only after I had confessed the whole truth about Carter Crenshaw. I had covered my ears as she whooped gleefully, "I knew, I knew it, I knew it!" Now her voice was calmer.

"Good news, Wendy. He said he would put it on the six and ten o'clock news tomorrow night. He even promised to get a camera crew over there to get some footage. He didn't sound too hopeful though. He said it was probably too late."

"Let's just not talk about it," Mickey warned me sixth period with an *I told you so* attitude.

"Fine," I answered him shortly. I wouldn't even tell about the TV coverage. I could play his game.

"You gonna walk home?" he asked me after class.

I gathered up my books and tried not to look at him. "No, I think I'll ride the bus today. It looks like rain." I wasn't trying to be cruel. I just didn't want to be with him. He actually seemed smug. Even though I had had lots of practice, I was really not a good loser.

"Are you angry with me, Wendy?" he asked, trailing beside me down the hall.

"No, Mickey," I lied. "I just don't want to walk through the park today. It would make me feel sad."

He stopped. "I understand," he mumbled. But I doubted that he really did.

Ted Carter's news story the next evening was brief, but honest and sympathetic. They had taken some pictures, and he explained about the petition, and the work, and the storm. Then he told about the city council meeting and made some remark about how economics always outweighed esthetics. I wasn't sure what he meant by that.

I don't know what I expected—lightning bolts with a revelation from heaven, or the phone ringing to hear the mayor apologizing, or people knocking on the door offering to help. I don't know what I expected, but there was nothing, just nothing. I went to bed, again unable to sleep.

Anxiety tugged me awake before dawn. It was Thursday. There was only one more day. I tried to rationalize myself into peace. If Mickey didn't care, why should I? It wasn't my neighborhood. I just wanted to forget and go back to sleep.

I ate lunch with Jane in the cafeteria. She was excited about the news coverage.

"I knew Uncle Ted would come through. It was so exciting. He even mentioned your name. Weren't you pleased with it, Wendy?"

Unenthusiastically I agreed that I was pleased and that it was well done. Even more than I had hoped for.

"Then why the gloomy face?" she demanded.

"I don't know, Jane. I guess I thought something would happen. I suppose it was too late. We should have done it sooner."

She tried to cheer me up. "There's no use crying over spilt milk," she argued with her undaunted optimism.

"I don't need cliches, Jane," I wailed. "I need help. It's the old recess syndrome, remember?"

She clucked sympathetically. "What you need," she suggested, "is a dramatic, last-ditch stand." She thought for a moment. "Like picketing the mayor's office with big signs. A demonstration might wake someone up."

She had hit the nail right on the head!

I looked at her excitedly. "No, not picketing the mayor's office, but what about a demonstration at the park itself?"

She eyed me quizzically. "What good would that do? No one would see it but the people in Crescent Heights and they can't do anything."

"But what if everyone saw it? Everyone in town?"

Jane was still confused. "How?"

"The TV!" I cried. "Jane, we'll have to talk to your uncle again. I know exactly what to do. It may not work, but it can't hurt."

I outlined my plan to her. It had come in such a flash that I knew it was rough, but just maybe things would fall into place.

The bulldozers were supposed to be at the park in the morning to begin ripping it apart and moving the earth out of the way.

"What if we were there first, a whole crowd of people with signs protesting, standing in the way so the machines couldn't move?" I asked, trying to keep my voice at a normal level.

Jane's eyes were wide. "Like Ghandi or Martin Luther King. Throwing our bodies into their path so they would either have to kill us or stop work? All right, Wendy!"

I tried to calm her down. "Well, maybe nothing quite as drastic as that, but that's the idea. We need the TV cameras there to get the pictures on the spot."

"Wait a minute! Wa-a-it a minute," she said. "I can't believe that *you* of all people—timid and shy and scaredy as you are—would actually do something like this. You, Wendy?"

I squared my shoulders and looked her straight in the face. "May I remind you, Jane, that 'God has not given us a spirit of fear but of power and love and a sound mind.' "

"May I remind you that I'm the one who reminded you of that in the first place?" she retorted. Then we both giggled.

"I'll talk to Uncle Ted again," she promised, "and I'll call the Project Outreach committee. I think some of them will help. But I don't know of anyone else. Our parents would never agree to it, would they?"

I didn't know. I knew it sounded crazy and wild, but I felt crazy and wild. I was willing to do almost anything to save that park and to prove that Mickey was wrong. My motives were confused, but I didn't stop to question them.

"I'll chain myself to the backhoe," Jane said dramatically. "Oh, I hope I get on TV. What do you wear to a demonstration, Wendy?"

Maybe her motives were mixed up too, but it really didn't matter now. If only I could get Mickey and Dad to agree to this.

I decided to try Dad first. He was hesitant.

"I don't know, Wendy. It sounds kind of dangerous to me. Kids running around with heavy machinery moving." He shook his head. "Besides, you need more people. How are you going to round up enough people at this date?"

"There's me and Jane and surely Mickey will help. He can get some others from his block."

"I'll do it," Cammie volunteered. I hadn't realized that she was standing there in the doorway of the kitchen listening. "And I'm sure Sean will too. I'll bet we can get him to make some signs and posters."

Dad was still doubtful. "Wendy, I really don't feel like I can give you my permission for this. I just have a funny feeling about it. It's too late, it's unorganized."

"Are you refusing to let me try?" I asked.

He sighed. "Not refusing, I guess. Just not quite giving you my blessing."

If Dad was hesitant, then I knew Mom would be adamant. I swore Cammie to secrecy. "Please don't tell Mom," I begged. "There's no need to upset her any more than we already have."

Cammie understood.

The next big hurdle was Mickey. I dreaded talking to him. My apprehension proved true.

"No, Wendy, it's dumb." He had met me at the Burger

Barn. "I don't want to get out there in public and make a fool of myself."

I had known he wouldn't like it, but I didn't expect him to be quite so hostile.

"Why can't you leave it alone?" he continued. "I told you from the beginning that it wouldn't work. You wouldn't believe me. No way am I going to get out there and parade around with a sign in my hand, and I won't ask anyone else to do it, either."

His eyes reflected stubbornness and pride, and his mouth was tightly drawn.

I couldn't think of anything more to say to convince him. I had presented my arguments as logically as I could. I had done my best to persuade him—even agreeing that it was the very limits of desperation, but it was no use.

"No," he repeated calmly and quietly, "I don't want any part of it."

"Then I guess I'll just have to do it without you." Dad had said I could be stubborn too.

"I wish I could stop you," he said angrily. "But I know I'd be wasting my breath. Why can't you leave us alone? No one asked you to stick your nose into this anyway. We were doing all right before you came along. We'll do all right without you. We don't need anyone to feel sorry for us."

Now I was angry, but I restrained the tremor in my voice. "That's true, Mickey. You don't need anyone to feel sorry for you. You're doing a pretty good job of that all by yourself."

Chapter Nineteen

I didn't need Mickey. I didn't need Dad. What was it Cammie had said about me? I did those things that no one else would do? Well, I would do it. For once I was not afraid of making a fool of myself. I might want to jump in the hole after the backhoe had finished and just let them cover me up, but I wasn't going to quit.

I knew now that it wasn't for myself. I had not forgotten what Dad had told me about being a disciple, about laying aside self for others. No, it was not for me. It was for Mom, for the people in Crescent Heights, and even for Mickey if he would only believe it.

It was nearly midnight before I felt we were halfway organized. I'll never know how we managed to do it without Mom finding out, but we did.

Ted Carter had agreed to have a TV camera on the scene by seven o'clock the next morning. Cammie came in late. She and Sean had made a half dozen posters and even had them nailed to long sticks. They were in Sean's car. He would meet us there at seven along with Troy and Ron. Cammie was going to drive me and Jane.

It didn't promise to be much of a demonstration, but it was the best we could do at short notice. Even I began to have doubts, but there was no stopping now.

I set my alarm for six o'clock and that night I slept.

The next morning's weather matched my mood, clear and cool. I woke Cammie up, and we dressed warmly and tiptoed downstairs. Jane was waiting for us on her front porch and I waved her over. We got in the car, and Cammie backed out of the driveway. No one was talking except Jane, of course.

"This is so exciting. Almost as exciting as getting my braces off. I hope we have a real crowd there."

I hated to dampen her enthusiasm by telling her that the "crowd" was right here in the car, so I let it pass.

When we reached the park, Sean was waiting with the signs in hand. Ron and Troy were there too. The car with Channel Four News painted on the side pulled right behind us.

Men dressed in work clothes and hard hats were driving stakes into the ground. The heavy earthmoving equipment was already in place.

"Well, Captain," Sean spoke to me. "What do we do now?"

Everyone waited for me to make some decision. I didn't even know where to start. One of the TV camera men came over to us. He rubbed his hands together to keep warm.

"I'm putting one camera here and we'll have the moving camera following you around and focusing on Mr. Carter too. How much time do we have?"

"Let's get the show on the road," chimed in Jane as she took one of the signs in her hand.

Cammie looked at me too. It was my ball game and I had to start calling the plays. I felt like running away instead.

Mr. Carter had arrived by now and walked over to us. "Where is everyone?" he asked innocently.

"I'm afraid that this is everyone," I admitted. "And I'm also afraid that I really don't know what to do next."

"Well, it's your show. The cameras are ready to roll," he said.

"Come on, Wendy," Cammie urged. "Let's do something even if it's wrong."

It was like storming the Bastille. We all picked up our signs and bravely marched right into the path of the machinery. One of the workmen was in the cab warming up the engine. Another ran over to us. I think he must have been the foreman.

"What're you doing here?" he yelled. "You'll have to get out of the way or you'll get run over. We have orders to start digging out this strip right now, right where you're standing." He was very agitated.

"We have no intentions of moving," I said defiantly, amazed at the strength in my voice. "We are here to protest the destruction of this park, and we have no intention of moving," I repeated, planting my feet firmly in the still damp earth.

I stood right in the middle of one of the spots where Dad had planted the grass seed. I looked down. I looked again. I could actually see minute, barely visible, but undeniable green sprigs of baby grass pushing their way bravely through the soil. It was all the sign I needed. I felt like Joan of Arc.

The cameras were rolling, and I could hear Ted Carter giving the usual TV spiel about on-the-spot news and explaining where we were and what we were doing and why.

"Look, lady, I don't know who you are or what crazy house you escaped from, but I've got my orders and you and your funny friends will have to get out of the way or we'll run right over you," the foreman threatened.

"Brutality!" Jane shrieked and moved over closer to me. "We're here in a peaceful demonstration. I defy you to move that thing one inch!" She pointed at the bulldozer with her sign.

The poor man didn't know he had unleashed a tiger in Jane. I almost felt sorry for him.

"I'll be—" He almost swore before he realized he was on TV. "I'm calling the cops and the mayor and the chief city engineer." He stomped away to his truck and began working a two-way radio.

I felt like whooping. The first victory was ours. Sean had his arms around Cammie, smiling. Jane was jubilant.

"Call the president of the United States, if you want to," she dared the workman, waving her poster wildly in the air.

Dear, beautiful crazy Jane. I could have hugged her.

"What now?" Cammie asked.

Mr. Carter answered. "Now we wait. If I guess right, there should be cars swarming all over the place pretty soon. In fact, here comes one now. Let's get a shot of this, Jim. There was the unmistakable sound of a police siren. I had never considered the fact that the police might be called in. The siren was loud enough to wake up half the people in Crescent Heights who began pouring out of their houses and heading toward the park. Mr. and Mrs. Webster were the first to reach us. Mrs. Webster still had her hair in pink rollers.

"Hey, girl," Mr. Webster yelled at me. "Let's give them what for. Why didn't you tell me what was going on? Think they can tear up this park? Nosiree. They've got another thing coming."

I was surprised to find Mrs. Decker standing beside me. I had not seen her approach the park. "Wendy, may I please have a sign?" she asked. As she took one in her hand, she smiled. "This is a brave thing you're doing. Mickey told me last night."

Then Mickey was there too, but he said nothing. Nor did he smile.

There were at least twenty people milling around by

now, and the cameras were on again broadcasting the escapade to the whole city. I only hoped someone was awake enough to see it and to care.

A big policeman climbed out of his car and sauntered over to us. "Who's in charge of this?" he demanded.

Everyone looked at me. "I am," I said quietly. I was not afraid.

Everything happened so fast after that, it's hard to explain. Another police car came up and then another car from one of the other TV channels. The whole park looked like it was swarming with policemen and cameramen. The city engineer drove up, then the mayor, and finally Mom and Dad! They were smiling, and Mom waved a piece of paper at me.

Dad hugged me really hard. "We've won, Wendy! We've won, at least temporarily."

Mom walked over to Mayor Dennison and the city engineer. They stood around and talked and frowned and gestured at the crowd and the machinery. She said something to the mayor and then handed the paper to him. The mayor didn't look happy as he read it.

"That's a temporary restraining order," Dad explained.

"A what?" I asked.

"It means that they can't do anything, at least for right now. It gives us our day in court," he replied.

I found out later that Mom had done it all. She had a friend who was a lawyer and also one of her customers at the gallery. Mom had convinced her to help and somehow she had gotten a judge out of bed to issue the necessary papers.

It was almost too good to be true.

"This isn't the end of it," Dad warned as Mom came over to us, and he put his arm around her shoulder. "This doesn't mean that the park is saved, but it does give us time to catch our breath and plan our next move. You were right, Wendy. The commissioners and mayor are answerable to someone. Now we can appeal to a higher court."

Elated is a poor word to describe how I felt. Mickey stood there beside me, silent and withdrawn.

"Let's go home and have some breakfast," Mom suggested. "I think we've done enough for one day."

"Dad, did you see the grass?" I pointed toward the spot where I had stood. It was trampled now, but the tiny sprigs miraculously were still there. "Look, the grass is coming up."

"So, it is," he said, beaming. "Someone has walked on it, but that won't stop it now. Grass is pretty tough—just like this park and the people of Crescent Heights."

"All but one, huh, Wendy?" Mickey said as he turned and walked away.

Mrs. Decker looked at me sadly. "His silly pride," she said and followed him down the street.

It had all happened so quickly. We went back home. Sean, Jane, Ron, and Troy came with us. Mom made pancakes and poured lots of gooey syrup on them. "It's a celebration, Rob," she said laughing. "We're entitled."

Dad just laughed too and helped himself to another stack.

It was great to have my family all together and laughing and caring again. We would be all right. The park would be all right. But what about Mickey? I wanted to rejoice and feel as happy as everyone else did. We had won, hadn't we? The taste of victory should be sweet, but it was bittersweet. It had been bought with an awful price if it meant losing Mickey.

Our Project Outreach fellowship was scheduled for the next night. I wasn't sure now that he would attend.

He came over that night, and we walked out to the gazebo and sat there. I wanted to hear him say it was all right, that nothing had changed, but he was quiet for a long time. Then at last he spoke.

"I've been ashamed to face you, Wendy," he admitted. "You were right and I was wrong. It doesn't do much good to say that now, does it?"

I didn't enjoy seeing him defeated and humbled.

"Just the fact that you've said it makes a difference, Mickey."

"What now?" he asked.

"I don't know," I confessed. I really didn't. Something had changed. I wasn't sure if it could be made right again or not.

"You feel like I've let you down, don't you?" Mickey asked. "That I wasn't brave enough or strong enough to do what had to be done?"

"Something like that, I guess." I hadn't been able to straighten it out in my own mind.

"I've tried to tell you all along that we were different. Two different worlds, two different ways of looking at things."

"But, Mickey, didn't today prove anything to you? People who care about others can overlook the diff—"

Gently he laid his fingers on my mouth.

"Enough preaching, OK, Wendy?" But it wasn't spoken in the sarcastic way he usually had.

"What I was going to say is that until now I never realized what that difference was."

I was puzzled, but I kept my mouth shut.

"You've tried to tell me all along, but I was too proud to listen. Then today, seeing you and your family and kids from the church doing all that for someone else, for Crescent Heights . . . . Well, it finally made me understand that you were right. I have been missing something in my life. It's just like you say, Wendy." He swallowed hard. "I need Jesus."

"Oh, Mickey!" My heart was so full of joy that I could hardly speak.

Then he finally smiled at me. Putting his arm around my shoulders he held me close. "Maybe we can start again. Forget about everything that's happened and just start over."

I grinned back and snuggled closer. "I think that's what it's all about, Mickey."